FAITH DEPARTED

ELIZABETH MADDREY

OTHER BOOKS BY ELIZABETH MADDREY

Hope Ranch Series

Hope for Christmas

Peacock Hill Romance Series

A Heart Restored

A Heart Reclaimed

A Heart Realigned

Arcadia Valley Romance – Baxter Family Bakery Series

Loaves & Wishes

Muffins & Moonbeams

Cookies & Candlelight

Donuts & Daydreams

The 'Operation Romance' Series

Operation Mistletoe

Operation Valentine

Operation Fireworks

Operation Back-to-School

The 'Taste of Romance' Series

A Splash of Substance

A Pinch of Promise

A Dash of Daring

A Handful of Hope

A Tidbit of Trust

The 'Grant Us Grace' Series

Joint Venture

Wisdom to Know

Courage to Change

Serenity to Accept

Pathway to Peace

The 'Remnants' Series:

Faith Departed

Hope Deferred

Love Defined

Stand alone novellas

Kinsale Kisses: An Irish Romance

Luna Rosa (part of A Tuscan Legacy)

Non-Fiction

A Walk in the Valley: Christian encouragement for your journey through infertility

For the most recent listing of all my books, please visit my website.

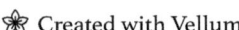

To all the women and men who suffer with infertility:
May the God of hope fill you with all
joy and peace as you trust in Him.
Even when it's hard.

1

"Stop stop stop stop." June breathed the words as the digital readout on the bathroom scale flickered up. She cringed when the hateful thing finally followed her directions. One forty. One hundred and forty pounds. She stumbled backwards off the scale and dropped onto the cold edge of the bathtub. At five foot two, she was used to numbers much more in the range of one ten. But the last six months had added thirty pounds...that was five pounds a month. She buried her head in her hands. What was going on?

"Morning, baby." Toby shuffled into the bathroom, rubbing his eyes. He stopped to give her an appreciative look and waggle his eyebrows. "Careful, you're going to make me late for work."

She chuckled in spite of herself. "You're insane." And blind. There was no point in drawing his attention to her ever expanding girth. She was on her way to being twice the woman he married four years ago. He hadn't signed on for a two-in-one special.

He grabbed her arm and pulled her close, burying his nose

in her neck. "I can't help it if I have the world's most enticing wife."

He couldn't possibly mean it. Her fat rolls squashed against his still-firm abs as he tightened his embrace. She fought the urge to push away and put on a robe. She forced her tone to be light. "Now, now. Didn't you say you had a big meeting this morning?"

He pressed a kiss to her head and eased back, eyes still hinting at his interest. "I did...sadly, I did."

She crossed her arms over her belly as he turned on the shower and tossed his towel over the door.

"Any news, June?"

She swallowed the lump in her throat and shook her head.

"We'll just have to practice more." He shot her a wicked grin and stepped into the steaming shower.

Nine weeks. She'd gone off her birth control pills nine weeks ago. Shouldn't something have happened by now? June padded into the walk-in closet and began to dress. Toby wasn't the only one with a big meeting today. She sucked in her stomach, hooked her favorite black dress pants, and slowly let out her breath. She was going to have to buy bigger clothes if she couldn't get at least five of these pounds off. Watching herself in the floor-length mirror on the wall, she gingerly lowered into a squat then stood and twisted at the waist. It wasn't comfortable, but no seams had popped and the fabric didn't look like it was straining. Grateful that the Weskit was back in fashion, June tugged on a purple silk blouse and snagged the suit's blazer from its hanger. She slipped her feet into a pair of killer purple leather peep-toe heels and smiled. The right outfit really did lift your spirits.

Toby let out a low whistle when she came back into the bathroom to do her hair. "Looking good, baby. You're going to kick some butt and take some names."

She laughed. "Or maybe convince the DARPA program

manager that we're totally capable of performing on this contract. That would be better than leaving heel prints on government behinds."

"What time are you meeting?" He glanced at her in the mirror as he dragged a comb through his hair.

"Two-thirty."

"I'll be praying."

"Thanks. Hey, you up for dinner with July and Gareth tomorrow night?" June set down her eyeliner and studied the light application of makeup. It was more than she usually wore, but when you were meeting with the person who was the deciding factor in awarding a contract—especially one your boss was adamant you win—you put your best foot forward.

"Sure. You know I love seeing Joo-lye and Gar."

June swatted his arm. "You know she hates that."

Toby grinned. "Not my fault your mother couldn't spell it J-u-l-i-e like a normal person."

She shook her head. June had definitely gotten the better deal when it came to names. Their mother must have still been under the influence of the epidural when she'd named them. Or something. Other than deciding to name her twins June and July, the woman was the most rational, unfanciful person she'd ever known. Then again, in her mother's bizarre logic, since June had been born right before midnight on June 30th and July had been born just after midnight on July 1st, maybe that *was* the only rational choice. At least it hadn't been August.

June stretched up and kissed her husband's cheek. "Gotta run. Call and tell me how your meeting goes. I love you."

"Love you, too."

~

JUNE HUNG her jacket over the back of her chair and sat. She snapped her laptop into its dock and scrolled through the calendar on her phone while the computer booted. Her morning was clear, though there were enough tweaks needed on the demo server that she'd have plenty to do. Particularly since the demo this afternoon was supposed to be the crowning achievement that clinched the contract. She'd fought to keep it off the schedule and in reserve—in case things weren't looking promising. No such luck. Her boss was determined and it simply didn't pay to ignore Bob when he got a bee in his bonnet.

After a quick scan of her email, June opened a window that allowed her to connect virtually to the demo machine. It was so much nicer to work in her office than in the lab where people were coming and going all the time. Since the demo wasn't classified, even though the project would be, she was going to take advantage of the opportunity to work in her office while she could. She'd be locked in the secure computer lab soon enough. She opened the email that listed all the tweaks needed on the demonstration and dragged it to her second monitor. She'd start at the top and work her way down. With any luck, she'd be too engrossed to dwell on the fact that she wasn't pregnant yet. Two months wasn't that long in the overall scheme of things. But she'd been so positive this was God's timing for them to start a family. Toby wasn't quite as convinced, but he was willing to see what happened and leave it in God's hands. June sighed a prayer for understanding. Was she completely off base?

A line of code zipped by, catching her attention. She scrolled back up and narrowed her eyes. Well, there was the cause of one problem. Possibly a few more. She glanced at the list of bugs and pursed her lips. Yeah. A few of those issues could definitely be tracked right back to this careless typo. She read the comment above the block of code and shook her head. Of course Anthony had programmed this segment. She was going to have to talk to Bob about him sooner than later. But for now...she scrolled to the right place in the code and began to type. Better to just fix it. She could worry later.

"Lunch?"

June leaned back in her chair, phone to her ear, and stretched. "Yeah. I could eat. What time is it?"

Her sister's laugh echoed down the line. "Almost one. I did manage to remember you have a big demo today, so I waited a little longer. But I'm starving."

"Give me ten minutes and I'll meet you at our usual spot." June set the phone back in its cradle and pressed her fingers to her eyes. A headache was brewing behind her left eye. It could be from staring at the computer screen all morning, but it was more likely from irritation at her useless co-worker. How did Anthony continually manage to hoodwink the upper management into thinking he knew what he was doing? And why was she always the one having to clean up his messes? Her stomach rumbled. Maybe the headache was low blood sugar.

She grabbed her purse and a protein bar from the box she kept in the same desk drawer. Maybe if she nibbled it slowly enough she'd feel full. The waistband of her pants was already digging into her flesh. She didn't need to add a real meal onto the misery. Checking to be sure she'd saved her work and logged out of the demo server, she headed for the elevator.

Pushing through the sparkling glass doors of her building, June breathed in the crisp autumn air. For the beginning of October, it was cooler than she expected in the D.C. area. She wasn't complaining. Summers around here were miserable, but the fall tended to make up for it. They'd probably end up with a few more sweltering days before much longer, but for now she was going to enjoy this little taste of heaven. Glancing both ways, she stepped into the street and hurried across, ignoring the light. No one really paid attention to the traffic signals in this part of Arlington. Not even the cars. It was every woman for herself. Skirting around a meandering group of office workers, June darted between two of the non-descript office buildings and emerged into a small stone courtyard. A fountain bubbled merrily in the center. The iron and wood benches around the perimeter were mostly empty. She spotted her sister and grinned.

"You beat me." June plopped onto the bench and pulled her protein bar from her purse.

July looked at the bar and raised a brow. "That's it? You can't be serious?"

June lifted a shoulder and struggled to keep defensiveness out of her tone. "Thirty pounds Jules. I'm eating less and what I do eat is healthier than I ever worried about before. Doesn't seem to matter—the scale just keeps inching up."

"Sorry. I wish I had an answer for you. Though it's kind of nice to know you're seeing what it's like to be the stocky one." July gestured to herself.

"Yeah, well, at least you have the height to carry it off. Besides, if I gain another twenty pounds I'm going to be raiding your closet, so you might want to think more carefully about that." June grinned and tore open the wrapper of her lunch. "What'd you bring?"

"I feel bad...I'll eat it at my desk later."

"That's silly. Just eat. I can drool and dream."

"If you're sure?" At June's nod, July unzipped the top of her insulated lunch bag and extracted a container of lasagna. "Gareth made it last night. I'm not sure what got him on this learning-to-cook kick, but I'm not arguing. You guys in for dinner tomorrow night?"

June would have to remember not to eat during the day tomorrow. Then maybe she could afford to partake of Gareth's latest concoction. "Looking forward to it. Especially if that lasagna's any indication of Gareth's progress. Anything new with you two?"

"Actually..." Excitement practically sparked out of July's eyes. "Gareth's finally on board with trying to start a family. So we won't be too far behind you two. Won't it be great for the kids to play together?"

"That's great." June chewed the faux-chocolate-covered lump in her mouth. Why couldn't it taste like something other than a crayon? "And you're not behind us at all."

"Still nothing?"

"Not unless you count the aforementioned thirty pounds."

"Sorry. But don't get discouraged yet. I was reading online last night and it seems like six months is more typical when you actually want to get pregnant."

"As opposed to...?"

"Teenagers who are desperate not to, I guess. I don't know." July shrugged. "Point being, you don't have anything to worry about."

"I guess."

"Hey. I know so." July slung her arm around June's shoulder and squeezed. "I know what'll cheer you up...wanna hear the latest from the oh-so-exciting world of your sister, CPA extraordinaire?"

"Of course I do." June laughed and pushed aside her worries.

"So then I had to reboot the server remotely and pull in the backup I kept on my laptop. Once that got restarted, the demo went fine. But Anthony better hope he doesn't run into me in the hall anytime soon." June tucked her feet under her and let her head flop back onto the sofa. It had been a long day, made even longer by the gross incompetence of her coworker.

Changing into her flannel pajama pants and a t-shirt had been bliss, especially around her waist where her slacks had left a deep impression. But she wasn't going to think about that right now.

Toby drew his eyebrows together. "Wait. He went back in right before the demo and rolled back all the changes you made during the morning? On purpose? Why?"

She waved a hand. "He gave some song and dance about how he'd been testing something and it crashed, so he restored from the backup. But I suspect he realized I was changing his code and got mad. He thinks that no one should ever fix anyone else's code. I tried asking him to take a look at problems in his code the first couple of times I had to work with him. But he never thinks his stuff is the problem, so I quit even mentioning it. It's easier to fix it myself."

"Do you think you'll get the contract?"

"Hard to say at this point. We did manage to do a successful demo. I'm hopeful that'll make the difference. But Bob's on a rampage. Thankfully, I'm not part of the group who're on his radar. How was your meeting?"

"Not nearly that exciting. We didn't have any demos today, just slide after slide after slide." He shuddered.

"Ooh. Deadly. Probably full of pie charts too, weren't they?"

He laughed. "Got it in one. But the customer seemed pleased, so that's really all you can hope for. At least we know we're not on the short list for having our contract cancelled."

"That's good." June shifted to rest her head on his shoulder. Was there anything better than hanging out and talking with Toby about whatever came up? Not to her—this was heaven. "I had lunch with July. She and Gareth are going to start a family, too."

Toby was quiet. What was he thinking? He still wasn't completely on board with the idea, but he wasn't reconsidering. Was he?

"Say something, Toby."

"That's good, I guess. I just..." He turned to meet her gaze. "That's not why we're thinking about it, is it? Because your sister is?"

"No. Of course not." June frowned. Why would he say that? When June had first brought up the idea, July and Gareth were firmly in the 'we're too young for kids' camp. Whatever had changed their minds, June's ache for a child had nothing to do with any of that. Why would Toby even think that?

"Okay." He sighed and ran his fingers through his hair. "I still feel like it's too soon to be doing this. We're only twenty-four, just getting a good foothold in our careers. Things are starting to take off and I don't know what kind of life we'd provide for a kid. I mean, we'll have plenty of food, but no luxuries. Particularly since you want to stay home. And I fully support that. But it'll cut our income in half."

"So? We have a good house. Sure, it's not huge, but it's enough for a family of three. Even four, honestly. And I don't want to be an old mom—I want to have kids while we're young and can keep up with them." She pulled her lower lip between her teeth. "Do you want to stop trying?"

He shook his head and pulled her close. "That's not what I said. Or meant. But I don't think we need to rush things along and I guess I worry about the pressure you'll feel if things work out quickly for your sister."

She opened her mouth to deny it, then snapped it closed. He might have a point. He probably did have a point. She'd had trouble in the past with tangles that cropped up from being a twin. Was this another example of that? She and July had been discussing kids for the last year. Was that what had kindled her desire to try? Had she mistaken her own stirring desire for God's prompting?

Toby kissed the top of her head. "What if we both try not to stress about it?"

"That's a plan." June tipped her head so their lips met. She wasn't going to let this become a problem between them. God was going to give them a baby. And when Toby held his little girl, well, he'd probably be convinced that it'd been his idea all along.

2
———

Toby stretched his legs out in front of him and watched his best-friend and brother-in-law man the grill. "June had me convinced we were going to be eating gourmet tonight. Even I can grill steaks."

Gareth chuckled. "Thought about it, but I couldn't face the grocery store on the way home from work. So it's steaks and salad, and maybe some biscuits. I left all that in July's capable hands."

"By which you mean you left the can of biscuits in her hand and showed her where to pull to get it open?"

"Something like that, yeah. How is it that one sister, one *twin* sister, learned to cook and the other is hopeless in the kitchen?"

Toby shrugged. "Mystery of the universe, I guess. On the other hand, when you have to produce birth certificates to prove to people that you're really twins, you're probably different enough that no one should be surprised."

"There's that." Gareth adjusted the knobs on the grill, lowered the hood, and sank into a chair next to Toby. "How are you navigating the current baby craze?"

Toby glanced over his shoulder to be sure the sliding door into the house was shut. The last thing he needed was for either sister to overhear this. "I'm trying to bite my tongue and ride it out. Is it wrong that I'm hoping it's a phase and they'll get over it?"

"If you're wrong, so am I. Though from what July said, I'm doing better at hiding my hesitancy than you are."

Toby winced. "What'd she say?"

"That June thinks you're not really interested in having kids and she can't decide if that makes her feel angry or guilty."

"I'm not uninterested. I'm just not..." Toby scanned the small backyard lined with tall trees that were starting to show their fall colors. Before long, the leaves would drop and he'd be able to see the other older houses that comprised the Bethesda, Maryland, neighborhood. July and Gareth had snagged the foreclosure for an incredible price three years ago. His search for the right word came up empty. "I don't know. I'm ambivalent, I guess. I hadn't been sitting around thinking about kids. They were still an abstract idea that fell into the category of 'someday.'"

"I don't think women have that category." Gareth stood and opened the grill. He poked the steaks with his tongs, prying up one end to peer under it.

"They should. What'd you tell July?"

"About what? When she asked about us having a family?"

Toby nodded.

"Being somewhat wiser in the ways of happy relationships than you, I said that if she thought it was a good idea, then I was on board." He flipped one of the steaks.

"So you're ready for a child in nine months?" Toby crossed his arms, frowning. It wasn't that he wanted to be at odds with June, but a solid marriage wasn't founded on the 'yes, dear' principle. If you had a differing opinion, didn't you owe it to yourself, and your spouse, to state it and then work to an agreement?

Gareth continued flipping steaks. "Nope." He closed the lid to the grill and turned to face Toby. "But the way I look at it, the chance of having a baby in exactly nine months is slim. Everything I've read..." he narrowed his eyes, "don't give me that look. I have a medical degree and I research for a living." He cleared his throat. "As I was saying, everything I've read says that three to six months is the average time it takes for couples to conceive, but that up to a year is still nothing to worry about. So will I be ready for a baby in twelve to fourteen months? More so than I am now."

"You don't think you should wait until you're ready?" Wasn't that the more responsible option? Being a father was such a big responsibility...you didn't just jump into something like that. Did you?

"In an ideal world, sure. But how do you even know you're ready? What does 'ready' mean?"

Toby frowned.

"Exactly. That's the very same eloquent response I came up with when July asked me those questions. Thus," Gareth spread his hands, "I'm on board. And praying fervently that God'll give me some time to get used to the idea before I have to start changing diapers."

Toby let out a short laugh. "That's a prayer I can get behind."

"Now, you want to let the girls know we're about five minutes out? These puppies are nearly done."

~

"YOU'RE QUIET AGAIN."

Toby glanced over at June and smiled. "Sorry. Combination of a good meal, good conversation, and trying my best to concentrate on this crazy Beltway traffic. Why is it always so much worse on the Maryland side of things?"

June laughed. "More Maryland drivers?"

"There's that, isn't there?" Toby accelerated and slid into the next lane to get around the contrary person doing forty-five. The blast of a horn behind him had him stomping the gas. When had fifty-five become the qualifying speed instead of the speed limit? "Did you make the dessert at July's? I didn't think your sister baked."

"She doesn't, usually. But peanut butter brownies are something she's always been pretty good at. Though in this case I did help."

"Did she send some home?"

June grinned. "She did."

Toby looked over as she lapsed into silence, staring out the passenger window. He laid his hand on her thigh. "You okay?"

"I guess. I'm..."

He waited several heartbeats for her to continue. As the silence lengthened, he prompted, "You're?"

She sighed and twisted in her seat, tucking one foot under her. "I've been thinking about what you said last night. About me wanting kids only because July does? Or at least because she and I have been talking about it. I guess I'm worried that you're right but that I'm not able to see it."

"Oh, baby. I didn't mean to make you worry like that." These were tricky waters. "If you've been thinking and praying about it then I don't think you're being influenced by your sister. And I'm sorry I put that thought in your head."

"The thing is, you might not be completely wrong. I can see where you're coming from, too, you know? It would be nice to know we're ready and to have every possible box checked before we had a baby. But once you start down that path, how do you know when you're done? Some boxes are always going to be there, no matter how much effort you put into trying to check them off. Right?"

He flicked on the turn signal and slid into the exit lane. It was a reasonable question. He didn't really have an answer for it, either. What were his conditions for being ready? Could he put them into concrete ideas instead of the instinctual panic that started to build when he thought about the responsibility of raising a child?

"I don't know. I haven't spent much time thinking about what 'ready' looks like. Tell you what, why don't we both take a few days to put together something concrete? Then we'll talk it over and see where we are. Wednesday date night?"

June nodded, a smile brightening her face. "Deal."

3

June waved to friends across the crowded foyer and tugged on Toby's hand.

"Come on, let's go say hi to Ginger and Martin." She wound her way through the crowd, dragging Toby along in her wake.

"Hi, June." Ginger grinned and pulled June into a fierce hug. "I've missed seeing you, where've you been? Hey, Toby. You remember, Martin, right?"

"Of course." Toby shook hands with Martin, dodging Ginger's enthusiastic attempt to hug him.

"We switched to a church that had a service on Saturday nights for a while. It was getting too hard to get up early that extra day. But neither of us could get over the fact that it doesn't feel like church on a Saturday night. As hard as it is to set an alarm and get out the door on Sunday mornings, I think we're both too conventional to do anything else."

Ginger laughed. "I'm too conventional to even try a Saturday night service, so you've got me there. Martin lobbied for it for probably six months before he finally gave up."

Martin shot Ginger a good natured smile. "I'll get you to one at some point. Now it's a challenge."

"Got any recommendations for small group classes? Part of our decision to try another church was feeling like we didn't really fit anywhere in the small groups." Toby checked his watch. "Either hour is fine since we're early enough."

"You remember Kevin McGregor?" When June nodded, Ginger continued. "You heard he and Lydia Brown got married, right?"

"Heard all about that, yes. And the stuff leading up to it. As much as I try to stay out of the gossip loop because it's a weakness for me, that whole story was hard to avoid." June pressed her lips together. "I still feel bad for Pastor Brown."

Ginger nodded. "Well, Kevin and Lydia started up a new small group not too long after they got married. It's got a pretty good mix of couples and singles, but it's definitely focused on Bible study and growth. We've been going there for, what?" She looked at Martin.

Martin scratched at his neatly trimmed goatee. "Hmm. Probably three months now."

"Is there room for more? The last small group June and I tried, the room was so full we ended up sitting on the floor in front of another couple. It might've been a good fit in terms of content, but since we didn't physically fit, we didn't see the point in trying it again."

"Ugh. We tried a few like that when we were looking. You'd think they'd stop listing it on the information sheet when they were at capacity. This one's not too full. It averages twenty people, but they meet in one of the large rooms upstairs in the education building and we could easily have twice that without it being uncomfortable." Ginger pulled an old bulletin from inside the front cover of her Bible and wrote on the corner. She ripped off the scribble and offered it to June. "That's the room number so you don't have to look it up. We're not staying today, but you should still go check it out."

"Speaking of which," Martin raised his eyebrows, "we should get going. Ginger's sister just had a baby and it's a mandatory family appearance for all to ogle and ahh over the newborn."

"Have fun." Toby grinned. "It was good to see you two."

"Call me later this week and tell me what you thought of class, okay?" Ginger pulled June into another hug before being led away by Martin.

June turned to Toby. "What do you think? Go to the service then give Kevin's small group a try?"

"Sounds good. Let's go get seats before we have to sit in the front row."

"I ALWAYS FORGET how big this building is." June glanced at the room number in her hand then at the sign on the wall with arrows pointing in various directions. Was there such a thing as a decent-sized church in terms of people without a building so enormous you could get lost in twenty seconds?

Toby pointed left. "This way, then right. I think the men's group I used to be in met in the same room. This seems familiar."

June grumbled under her breath. Of course it seemed familiar. It *all* seemed familiar. It was one familiar hallway after another, all lined with familiar classrooms full of people of various ages. It was like that text-based adventure game for computers her dad tried to get her to play when she was in high school. He'd said the retro experience would be good for her. Like anyone interested in computers would willingly go back to a command line gaming experience.

"Here we go." Toby stopped in front of the room and

gestured for June to go in.

Sometimes chivalry wasn't all it was cracked up to be. Why did she have to be the first to go in? June took a moment to push her lips into a smile before grabbing Toby's hand and stepping in, stopping to the right of the doorway. She let her gaze roam the room. Was there anyone she knew? Or even recognized? She paused when she saw a petite brunette. Linda? Leslie? No. Laura.

Toby leaned down to whisper in her ear. "Recognize anyone?"

"Think so. See the brunette? That's Laura...something. She almost lived in the townhouse with July, Ginger, and me when we first moved out here. Don't remember what happened, but she didn't end up as a roommate. Though she's always been friendly when I've run into her."

"That's a start...looks like she's coming this way." Toby straightened and slipped his arm around June's shoulder.

"Hi." Laura tilted her head to the side. "June, right?"

June nodded.

Laura grinned. "I thought you looked familiar. Haven't seen you around for a while, but it's great to have you back. Are you going to join our small group?"

"Trying it out, at least. Ginger said she and Martin have been coming and enjoying it. We're just switching back to Sundays from Saturday night. This is my husband, Toby. I don't think you've met."

"Don't think so, no." Laura grinned and shook Toby's hand. "Nice to meet you. Come on in, you two, find a seat. I'll introduce you around."

June and Toby followed Laura around the room. It was a bit like being towed behind a whirlwind. Laura knew everyone and rattled off their names and pertinent details so quickly June was never going to remember a tenth of it. Before long, they were seated and Kevin was opening the class in prayer.

The class was good. More than the touchy-feely groups they'd been visiting lately. It was nice to have people pose deeper questions, and to have others in the class actually give serious thought to their answers. Was Toby enjoying it as much as she was? June snuck a look to her right. He appeared focused and seemed to be interested. That was a good sign. Maybe finding a small group wasn't going to be as tedious as either of them had thought.

When they started going around the circle taking prayer requests, June sucked her lower lip between her teeth. Should she mention starting a family? True, she didn't know that many of the people here, but having more prayer would be good. Wouldn't it? She flicked her gaze to Toby again. On the other hand, he'd be annoyed. Oh, he wouldn't say anything about it most likely, but he'd sigh and give her that look. The one that made it clear he thought she worried too much. Which she did.

The woman next to her gave an expectant look and June shook her head. Was she imagining it, or did Toby exhale? It was good she hadn't said anything. Better to wait 'til they knew more people anyway.

When the class was over, they mingled for a few minutes before heading to the car.

"What'd you think?" June clicked the buckle of her seatbelt and turned to look at Toby.

"It's nice to be back. I'd forgotten how much better a preacher Pastor Brown is than most. For that matter, Kevin's a good small group leader. I'm game to go back to that group and give it another few weeks to see how we settle in. What about you?"

June grinned. "Basically the same as you. That was easy."

"So it was." Toby returned her grin and backed out of the parking spot. "Now, since we have a lovely autumn afternoon, what would you like to do?"

4

June dashed across the busy Arlington street, giving a friendly wave to the car blaring its horn, though they'd been in no danger of hitting her. They hadn't even needed to slow down. It had been clear that July was bursting with news when she called to make sure they were still on for lunch. Why couldn't July have given her a hint? Being kept in the dark was aggravating. Which was probably why July did it so often. Little sisters, even those who were only ten minutes younger, were a pest.

"Where's your lunch?" July frowned as June sat beside her and fanned her face vigorously.

"Not hungry. Besides, it's Friday. Toby wants to go out for dinner. I'd rather save my calories for that. I thought it was October. Where did this heat wave come from?"

July laughed. "You know we always get one last reminder of what summer's like before it settles into fall. This is it. But I'm not going to let the eating thing go. What's the deal?"

"Are you blind? Look at me." June stood and turned to the side, pulling her baggy shirt so it was snug around the growing pooch of her belly. "I gained two more pounds last week, despite my best efforts. I'm going to have to start running or something." She gave a shudder. At this rate, she'd be shopping in the Women's section by Halloween. And she'd probably need to get everything tailored. Did they do petite fat clothes? She didn't want to find out.

"You should keep a food diary. That helped me when I..."

June held up a hand and slid her phone out of her pocket. She navigated to the main screen, gesturing to the icon for a popular calorie-tracking app. "Want me to add you as a buddy? Maybe you can figure out what I'm doing wrong. I'm practically a vegetarian. Lots of whole grains and vegetables, low fat. And right at the lowest number of calories deemed acceptable, if the various fitness sites online are to be trusted. Plus I drink so much water I lose an hour of productivity each day to bathroom trips."

"Sorry." July frowned and patted her sister's leg.

"No. I'm sorry. You said you had news and I'm rambling about being fat. What's going on?"

July's face split into a grin and she leaned in, her voice dropping to a whisper. "I think I'm pregnant."

June blinked. Her heart sank into her stomach as she tried to wrap her mind around the words. "But...you said...you just..." Her sister's expression penetrated the confusion and June forced a smile. "That's great. I'm just surprised. I thought you only decided to try last week though."

July hunched her shoulders, looking like a child caught with her hand in the cookie jar. "I never could figure out how to tell you we were trying too. It never seemed like the right time. Whenever I started to tell you, you were struggling with disappointment and I couldn't decide if you'd be mad. We actually made the decision about two weeks before you did, but Gareth didn't want me to tell anyone. Not even you."

June's jaw sagged open. There had been a number of things in their marriage that Toby had asked her not to tell anyone, including July, but June had always insisted that she couldn't *not* tell her twin. They were more than simply sisters. Weren't they? But now...maybe she'd been wrong. She cleared her throat. "How far along?"

"A few weeks. I took the test on Sunday."

"Sunday." July'd waited a whole week to tell her. Or most of a week. "I see."

"Don't be like that." July crossed her arms. "I told you before anyone else. Well, not Gareth, obviously. And Mom."

June's eyebrows shot up. "Mom knows already? Great. Thanks. Glad I at least made the top three." She pushed off the bench and scowled at her sister. "I see that I need to readjust my thoughts on how our relationship works these days. That'll make Toby happy, at least, since I always used to refuse to promise not to tell you. I *thought* you did the same." She took a few steps then stomped back. "I am happy for you, if you're actually interested in my congratulations. Seeing as I'm so far down in your list of people who matter."

July flinched. A tiny spear of pleasure bloomed in June's heart as the barb hit home. She turned and stalked back to her office.

⁓

"A WEEK, TOBY." June threw her shoe into her closet. "How do you wait a week to tell someone something like that?"

Toby perched on the edge of their bed, face impassive. "Maybe she was worried about your reaction? Can't imagine why, of course."

June sighed and kicked her other shoe in the general direction of the first. At least this one didn't dent the wall. She crossed the room and flopped face-down on the bed. "I'm being a beast, aren't I?"

Toby lay back, turning so his nose touched hers. "Maybe a

little. Though I guess I understand. Not completely. The twin thing has always boggled me, but I try to roll with it. Honestly, what seems weirder to me is that she waited so long to tell you they were trying. And, if I had to guess, it's the speed that one followed the other that's really upsetting you."

She closed her eyes. Was that the problem? She and Toby had been trying to start a family for ten weeks without anything to show for it, unless you counted stretch marks and a closet full of too-tight clothes.

"You might be right."

Toby kissed her nose then sat up. "I often am."

June snorted. "Keep telling yourself that."

"Regardless. Try to remember that they're firmly in the four-months-of-trying category, so well within average, even if it feels like it's only been a week. We're not there yet. Besides, it's not a race." He slapped her behind with affection. "So why don't you call and make up with your sister and then we can go out to eat."

Groaning, June flipped over. "Fine. But choose someplace that has salads."

Toby frowned. "You don't need to lose weight. You're beautiful."

"Salad." June sat up and shooed at him.

Shaking his head, Toby wandered out of the room. June watched him leave and smiled. After all their years together, just being near him still gave her heart a little jolt. She'd figure out what to do about him being blind later. For now, it was enough that he loved her. Even if she was fat.

She reached for the phone with a sigh. Better to get it over with.

~

"You need to apologize to your sister."

June closed her eyes and took a deep breath before she tucked the phone between her shoulder and her ear so she could continue folding laundry. "Hi, Mom. I'm fine, thanks. How about you?"

"I'm fine, June. But you need to apologize to July."

"I already did, not that I really think it's any of your business."

Her mother huffed out a breath. "Of course it's my business. Your sister's very upset."

"Theoretically that should be in the past tense since she assured me that we were okay when I talked to her last night." June dropped the shirt she was trying to fold and pushed the pile of laundry aside so she could sink onto the bed. Why had her sister said anything to Mom in the first place? Weren't they past the age of running to Mom every time they had an argument? She rubbed her temples as they began to throb.

"Fine. Though I don't really understand how you could be so mean in the first place. Here your sister tells you some exciting news and all you care about is that you weren't the first to know?"

"No, Mom, that's not it at all."

"Well what is it then, June?"

June hunched her shoulders. How was it possible her mother still made her feel like a misbehaving child? "She and Gareth started trying to get pregnant and she never said one word to me, though apparently she told you. Even when I told her we were starting to try, which would've been a natural time to mention it, nothing. Zip. And apparently she'll tell everyone *but* me and swear them to secrecy. I don't understand when we started not telling each other everything. Because *I* never got that memo and I haven't been the one holding out. Plus, since we're on the subject, I know for a fact that everything I say to you gets back to her. But you'll keep her secrets from me? How fair is that?"

Silence stretched across the phone line. June squeezed the bridge of her nose. She should've kept her mouth shut. Her mom was, obviously, upset now. Making June, as always, the bad guy in the situation. Nothing she did was right when it came to her relationship with her mother. Was that why she continued to feel obligated to tell Mom everything? What did she hope to prove?

"I'm sorry you feel that way. It certainly wasn't my intention to make you think I wouldn't keep your secrets."

June bit back a sigh. There it was: the guilt. The words seemed innocuous enough, but the tone...she shouldn't fall for it. But the urge to figure out how to make it better was already stirring in her chest. No. She wasn't going to play this game anymore. "Well then, Mom, you can start proving that now. Don't tell July about this conversation. Any of it."

"But, June, don't you think your sister deserves to know how you feel?"

"I already talked to her, as I've said to you three times now. So she knows how I feel. Stay out of it, Mom."

"All right. If that's what you want."

June squashed the blossoming tendril of guilt at her mother's latest sally. "It is. So, what's new with you and Dad?"

5

"How did it get to be November already?" June tugged her coat tighter. They were going to have to figure out their indoor spot soon. Fifty-six degrees was right on the edge of what she was willing to brave for any extended period of time. And that was only because it was sunny.

July rubbed her hands together then stuffed them into the pockets of her fleece pullover. "I have no idea. I'm also not sure how it's time for my first official doctor visit next week. I haven't been since that first week when the nurse did a blood test and gave me basic information...this makes it feel so much more real."

June fought the urge to flinch at the familiar twist under her breastbone. She was doing better with her sister's pregnancy, but there were moments—lots of moments—when it was still hard. She was learning to keep her mouth shut. Still, it wasn't feeling real yet? That seemed ridiculous. July had a life growing inside her. How did that not feel real? Let alone the subject of July's constant nausea that got wormed into every conversation. At least twice. With effort, June pushed her lips into a smile.

"Maybe she can give you something for the nausea. Or at least let you know if it's normal to be that sick all the time."

July narrowed her eyes. "Is that a backhanded way of saying I complain too much?"

"I'd never say that." Not out loud, at least. "I'm sorry. I'll stop talking about it with you."

June scoffed. "You're welcome to try, but I know you won't. And really, I'm okay with that. It's hard sometimes, I'll give you that. But you're my sister, Jules. Of course I want to talk about it with you. Just keep in mind that someday, hopefully someday soon, you're going to hear me gripe incessantly about how I can't stand this smell or that one and so forth and so on."

"I'm not *that* bad."

June pulled one hand out of her coat pocket and patted her sister's knee. "You go right on thinking that."

July laughed. "All right, all right. I'll try to keep an eye on it. So what's your big news? You *are* the one who called this little meeting. On a Monday, even, instead of our usual end-of-week recap gathering."

"First off, we got the contract." At July's quizzical look, June arched a brow. "From early October? Demo that Anthony the Useless nearly tanked?"

"Oh, that contract...I figured you got that a while ago. You're just *now* hearing back?"

June nodded. "The wheels of the government churn s-l-o-w-l-y. But, in appreciation of my efforts to save the day, I got a really nice bonus this morning. And Bob is making noises about promoting me, officially, to team lead as well as making me the Principal Investigator for the project."

July clapped her hands before leaning forward to squeeze June's shoulders. "That's great. Congratulations."

"Thanks. I'm a little nervous about the extra responsibility. I mean, right now I end up re-doing a good bit of the big A's code. But if I'm in charge of the team...I don't think I'll still have the time to do that, plus my own coding, plus the few managerial type things I'll have to do. Throw in being the PI...it's like I'm actually a grown up with a grown up job."

Chuckling, July patted June's arm. "You'll be great. But I understand what you're saying. When I landed the account for the hotel chain last year? I nearly choked every time I had to audit their books. Little businesses? No problem. But a major national corporation...it's still a little scary. I worry that I'm going to find someone embezzling from them. And then I worry that someone is embezzling but I'm *not* finding it."

June grinned. "Strangely, that makes me feel better." She glanced down at her phone to check the time. "I should run—meeting with Bob in about twenty minutes—but I needed to share the news with someone."

"Couldn't get a hold of Toby?" July poked out her lower lip in a mock pout.

"Nope. So you had to do."

"Brat."

"Uh, hello? Older sister? Later."

July shook her head and waved goodbye.

June hurried back to her office through the crisp air. She was late. Not for her meeting with Bob, she had plenty of time before that. Why hadn't she mentioned it to July though? Pausing at the corner to wait for the crossing light she pursed her lips. She wasn't entirely sure...though a small part might simply be not wanting to share immediately since July hadn't. And that was petty. And childish. With a sigh, she stepped off the curb and dashed across the street. Apparently she was both of those things, without much regret about it.

Of course, the pregnancy test she'd taken that morning had been negative. It was simply too early, right? Even if the test packaging bragged of its effectiveness up to a week before you were late. Not everyone produced pregnancy hormones at the same rate—that's why there were ranges. She'd wait a day or two then test again. And if it was still negative? She'd go get a blood test. Either way, she wasn't telling anyone, not even Toby, until she had something official to share. For now, she'd focus on the promotion. It was a good thing. If she told herself that enough, maybe she'd believe it.

~

JUNE SET her laptop on the storage bench they kept right inside the garage door and kicked her shoes underneath it. She hung her coat on one of the hooks and looped the strap of her purse over it. "Tobe? I'm home."

"Upstairs."

With a tired smile, she angled through the kitchen to the stairs and trudged up to their bedroom. She dug the folded promotion and bonus letters out of her back pocket then scooted onto the bed next to him. Lying back, she dropped the letters on Toby's chest. "What time'd you get home?"

"Mm. Maybe ten minutes ago? I just needed to stretch out for a minute or two. Long day." His eyes flicked to the papers. "What's this?"

"Open them and see." June wormed closer. When he shifted, she rested her head on his shoulder. Warmth rushed through her as Toby's arm tightened around her and he rubbed her shoulder.

"Mysterious." He shot her a grin and shook the first letter open, his eyes widening as he read. "Wow. Congrats, baby." He kissed her forehead. "My wife, the PI."

June laughed. "That sounds like I'm going to be chasing down bad guys and tip-toeing into not-quite-legal activities in the name of a good cause, not cracking a whip over Anthony's head and praying I don't have to officially recommend he be let go."

Toby rubbed her arm. "You'll be great. Who else is on your

team? Maybe you can delegate one of them to be his babysitter."

"Yeah, that thought occurred. I'm still trying to decide on the right choice." She flipped through the six people on her team and frowned. None of them were really all that fabulous. They did good work as a whole, but individually...not a single go-getter in the bunch. Yay for her. "The more I think about it, the more I realize the promotion's less of an honor than I originally thought. I don't think they had any other viable options."

"They can't be that bad." Toby shook his head and unfolded the other paper. He let out a low whistle. "That's a nice addition to the vacation fund. Way to go."

June grinned. She'd let him ear mark it vacation money for now. But it was going to be mostly spent on baby things. Their little townhouse might only have two bedrooms, but you could decorate a nursery in such a way that it'd grow with the baby. And if they ended up with more than one child in the long run...well, they could either share a room, or she'd talk Toby into moving. He loved being right off the highway and near Shirlington. So did she, for that matter. But there were houses in the area too, and since the real estate bubble popped right before they bought their current home, well, they might actually be able to afford one.

"What's for dinner?" Toby wiggled his shoulder, bouncing her head.

"Ugh. Why does dinner come around again every night?"

Toby laughed. "It just does. Get up and fix me food, woman."

"Watch yourself, buster, or I might put you in charge of dinner."

"Pizza it is."

"Good grief. Let me change and I'll go see what we've got." June rolled off the bed and unhooked her pants. Even her 'roomy' pants were feeling snug these days. It'd be absolute bliss to get into her soft, elastic-waist pajamas. At least the scale hadn't inched up this week. Yet. With a sigh and a firm mental shake, she hung up her work clothes, sorting through ideas for healthy, lower calorie meals that might come out of their refrigerator.

SHE WAS GOING to kill him. Her fourth full day as a team lead and June was ready to throw in the towel if it meant she never had to deal with Anthony again. The man was a menace. There was no other possible word to describe him. Trying to school her features as her blood pounded in her ears, she tapped on Sean's doorframe.

The IT guy looked up and pushed away from his computer. "Uh oh. I know it's bad news if you come get me. Usually you can figure things out on your own."

June managed a humorless laugh. "On the plus side, you don't actually have to go anywhere...I just need a backup restored."

"You can do that from your desktop, can't you? I'm pretty sure you have access to the backup server." Sean shifted and began to type on a different keyboard.

"Yeah...that's not going to help any. I need it restored from the tape. I'm really hoping there's a tape."

Incredulity spread across his face. "How'd you manage to delete the backup from the main backup server? That's...a challenge."

"Wasn't me. I'm trying to undo the damage before it's too late." June stuffed her hands in her pockets. "Please tell me there's a backup of the backups."

Sean studied her a moment before giving a slow nod. "Should be. It's simply a matter of finding it. Might not be local. How far back do you need?"

"As recent as possible. Far as I can tell, he did the deletions this morning and creamed the backups when he was trying to undo it. I'm really hoping we didn't lose much."

"Anthony."

It wasn't a question. June nodded. Did everyone know how useless Anthony was? Why was he still here?

"Leave me info on the files you need and I'll see what I can do."

"You're a life saver, Sean."

He grinned. "Don't forget it. And if you get a chance to spill coffee or kick him...do it for me, would you?"

"If only." June chuckled and headed back down the hall to her office. One down, too many to count remaining. She needed to type up this latest incident. If there was any hope of getting rid of him, documentation was going to be critical. Ignoring the rapid blink of her desk phone's message light, she opened a new file and began to type, detailing the loss of data —thankfully this time it was only test data, not the classified data they'd be dealing with when they were out of the prototype stage. Since she was at it, she outlined the issue with the customer demo in October as well. Should she mention how much clean-up she'd had to do to get the demo in workable order? June drummed her fingers on the keyboard. It was tempting. But inept wasn't really the same as destructive. She'd leave it out for now.

With the file saved, she punched the voicemail button. The blinking light was making her crazy. Why couldn't people just send an email?

"June? It's Jules...I need you. Call me back. Please?"

The timestamp indicated the call had come in...she glanced at the clock on her computer, twenty minutes ago. She winced. She should have listened to the voice mail first. She dialed her sister's cell number and berated herself for being so absorbed by teamwork idiocy. The call went to voice mail.

June hung up and dialed again.

"June?"

"Hey, July. Sorry, things here are crazy. Are you okay? What's going on?"

Her sister sniffled. "I...can you come to our spot?"

June checked the clock again. It was almost time to head home and there were a million things to do. Untangling the colossal mess her lovely team member made had eaten up her day. But this was July. "Yeah. I'll be right there."

June grabbed her purse and texted Toby to let him know she was going to be late tonight as she dashed toward the elevators. She waved off the two coworkers who tried to grab her attention. She'd be back. A mixture of worry and fear gnawed her gut. July hardly ever cried. And she never left ambiguous messages. She was the queen of the so-detailed-there-was-no-need-to-call-back voicemail. Something was definitely wrong. Was it Gareth? Or Mom?

Traffic on Fairfax Drive was thick with people leaving work for the day. June stabbed the walk light button and tapped her foot. As soon as the light changed, she darted into the street, dodging a car that ran the light. She shot the driver a murderous glare. Weaving nimbly through the sea of people swarming toward the Metro station, she skidded around the corner to the courtyard where she and her sister always met. July was hunched on a bench, arms wrapped around herself.

"July?" June hurried across the empty courtyard and sat. Her sister launched herself into June's arms, sobbing. What was going on? June wrapped her arms around July. "Shh...shh. What is it?"

"I...cramps...then...he's...she's...gone...gone."   July hiccupped and buried her face in June's shoulder.

What was she talking about? June tried to piece together the snuffled words into some kind of coherent sentence but came up blank. Wait. Everything in her seemed to plummet to her toes. Did she mean *the baby*?

"Jules...are you sure?"

July nodded, red-rimmed eyes still brimming with tears.

"Should you go to the doctor? Maybe...maybe it's a normal part of pregnancy?" Hadn't she read that sometimes you felt cramping during implantation? But July was too far along for that. And there could be spotting through the whole first trimester...right? Should she mention that? Her sister was every bit as much of a researcher as she was though. It was unlikely that July hadn't already considered, and rejected, the possibilities.

Swiping her arm across her nose, July shook her head. "Not like this. It was..." She gulped. "Just trust me...it isn't normal."

June gnawed on her lip. "I'm so sorry."

July managed a weak smile. "I don't know how I'm going to tell Gareth. He was getting so excited...my first doctor's appointment was next week. He kept going on about hearing the heartbeat on the Doppler. Now that appointment will be a follow up to make sure everything...passed."

June nodded. What was there to say? She didn't have any experience with pregnancy, so how could she even guess what a miscarriage was like? "What can I do?"

"Just pray. I...I should go. Maybe the office has cleared out enough that I can get my stuff and get home. When I realized what was happening, I just ran out of there."

June rubbed her sister's knee. She needed to say something else, didn't she? The words wouldn't come. "Call me if you need anything. Okay? I can come over...or bring dinner. Whatever you need."

"Thanks." July gave June a tight hug. "Love you, Sis."

"Love you, too."

June watched her sister hurry across the courtyard on her way back to her office. This was terrible. What must her sister be going through? At least now she wasn't going to be left as far behind when it came to starting a family. It wasn't a race. It wasn't...but still, she'd wanted to be first. She was older, even if it was only by a few minutes.

What was wrong with her?

6

July forced her mind to go blank. She wasn't going to think about it. She couldn't. What she needed to do was get her purse and laptop and get to her car without running into anyone. Her face was probably blotchy. Her face always got blotchy when she cried. Her eyes were most likely swollen, too. She was tall, stocky, and red-headed...why couldn't she at least cry prettily?

She peeked out the elevator doors. No one was immediately visible. So far, so good. Now, of course, she had to pay for wanting a nice view and dart down the long side of the building before she could get to her office. When she'd first been hired, her office had been three doors down from the elevator. On any other day, she'd have said the trades she'd made to move to her current office were completely worth it. Not today.

Taking a deep breath, she turned the corner and scurried to her office. The building was silent. Eerily so. Seeing as everyone went home early on Fridays when they could get away with it, there was no reason for her to sneak. But she couldn't stop herself. She hadn't told anyone at work she was pregnant. She certainly didn't want to have to explain the situation now.

With her laptop and purse safely in hand, she dashed back to the elevator and jabbed the button for the garage level. If she could get to her car she'd be home free. Then she'd have to figure out how to tell Gareth. A tear escaped and she hastily wiped it away. Two more floors. Why couldn't the elevator hurry?

Finally, the doors slid open. The garage was all but deserted. July jogged to her car, tossed her bags into the passenger seat, and laid her head on the steering wheel as tears began, once more, to flow. A scream lodged in her throat. Why would God give her a baby—one that was so desperately wanted and loved—only to take it away before it had any sort of chance to live? Was it because she'd kept secrets from her sister? No. God didn't work that way. Did He? No. Of course not. Then why? The question continued to echo, unanswered, as she started her car and headed home.

GARETH'S CAR was already in the driveway when July pulled in. Why couldn't he have been late tonight of all nights? She needed a minute, or twenty, to get herself together. Now there'd be no putting off the conversation. At least she'd stopped herself from calling her mom. June wouldn't say anything to anyone until she got permission. Her mother, on the other hand, would've been on the phone to Gareth as soon as they hung up. That was unfair. Mom could keep a secret when she worked at it. Mom hadn't told June that she and Gareth were trying to start a family. Of course, look where that had gotten them.

July winced as she leaned over to grab her things. These cramps were worse than anything she was used to. Was it because she knew what was going on? Did heartache intensify physical pain? Hands full, she used her upper arm to dry a fresh bout of tears. Trudging up to the kitchen door, July struggled to find the words she'd need. But only random, incoherent thoughts swam in her mind. Unlike June, Gareth was going to need her to explain, in detail, how she knew what was happening. The memory of the sharp cramp and unmistakable rush of blood caused an involuntary sob.

The door swung open. Gareth's face morphing into dismay as he looked at her.

"What's wrong? What happened?" He reached out, taking her bags and setting them on the floor before pulling July into the kitchen and his arms.

July's barely maintained control snapped and her knees buckled. She fell into his arms, sobbing.

"Are you hurt? Do you need a doctor? Was there an accident?" Gareth's rapid fire questions bounced off her. All she could do was shake her head. "Is it June? Your parents? Sweetheart...you've got to tell me what's wrong...you're scaring me."

July drew in a shuddering breath and looked up. Tears coursed down her cheeks, a watery echo of the shattered pieces of her heart. "I lost the baby."

GARETH HADN'T SAID ANYTHING. He'd just held her until she had, once again, gotten a semblance of control back. Then he'd nudged her upstairs and into a hot shower. When she emerged, her insides hollow, but at least no longer on the verge of tears, he'd bundled her into bed and brought up a tray with hot tea and chicken chili in a sourdough bowl. Clearly, he'd darted out to Panera while she was showering. How long had she stood there, letting the drops of hot water pound her into fragile serenity?

Now, also clad in his pajamas, he slipped into bed next to her with his laptop and another tray holding soup. "I figure something funny is in order. So...pick your chick flick and we'll stream it and eat soup."

July looked at him and smiled. He was such an incredible man. Questions lurked in his eyes, but he was holding them back, taking care of her instead. "What about the latest Die Hard? Then we get humor and explosions...everyone wins."

"Really?" The hope in his voice made her chuckle.

"Really. I'm actually not in the mood for sappy romance. Explosions sound like the perfect thing."

He frowned and sent her a long look. Apparently satisfied that she wasn't settling for something he'd enjoy, he nodded and got the movie set up.

"You want to eat and then start, or start while we eat?"

July shrugged. "Either."

Gareth used his remote to dim the lights and settled the laptop between them. After hitting play, he reached over and squeezed her hand. "Let the mindlessness begin."

JULY CLAWED her way out of sleep to escape the swirling black pit that had chased her through her dreams. Her heart pounded against her ribcage and she tried to swallow, but her desert-like mouth had no moisture to spare. She rubbed her eyes hard enough to leave spots dancing on her eyelids, then pushed herself up. The glowing numbers of the alarm clock across the room taunted her. Just a few minutes after six a.m., too early to get up, too late to bother trying to get back to sleep. She rubbed her arms as goose bumps rose on her skin. She didn't want to risk the dream again anyway.

Carefully, she slid her legs out of the bed, groping with her feet until they found her slippers. Rustling the covers as little as possible, she eased from bed with a slight smile for Gareth. He snuffled and flopped to his side, his breathing drifting into the deep rhythm of peaceful sleep. Lucky man.

She pulled the bedroom door closed behind her and tiptoed downstairs. She kill for a cup of coffee, why was it on the taboo list for pregnant...she stopped mid-thought and gripped the handrail. She could have coffee now. This was a positive thing. She'd make herself a big mug of coffee, maybe even break out the espresso machine. Her stomach twisted, acid oozing up her throat. Maybe not espresso.

In the kitchen, she laid her hand on the outside of the coffee pot. It was hot. Gareth must have set up the auto brew before bed. When did he have time? She'd enjoyed the soup in bed last night, and the movie...had she fallen asleep before it was over? Obviously Bruce Willis had somehow managed to save the day, it was a Die Hard movie after all, but the details were missing. She must've drifted off. Which explained why she was up so early. Well, that and the nightmare.

The unremitting darkness started to push its way into her mind but July fought it back. She might not be able to escape the nothingness in her dreams, but she wasn't going to be subject to it when she was awake. No matter what it felt like, her world hadn't ended. Maybe if she said it enough she'd believe it.

Gareth shuffled into the kitchen, his robe dangling untied, sandy brown hair tousled. He let out a jaw-cracking yawn as his gaze drifted to the coffee July had poured. "Morning...that for me?"

"Nope. But I'll get you some. You didn't have to get up."

Lifting a shoulder, Gareth settled at their kitchen table. "Don't want you to drink all the coffee."

July managed a weak smile as she dumped sugar into his mug. She carried both over to the table and sat.

"You okay?"

July blew across the top of her coffee. No, of course she wasn't okay. But saying it seemed harsh. "Not yet."

He covered her hand with his and squeezed. "I'm so sorry, baby. I don't..."

She flipped her hand over and laced her fingers through his. "I know. It's okay. We're okay. I'll...be okay." Someday.

"Did you sleep well at least? You seemed exhausted after dinner. Either that or you find exploding cars and dodging Russian police very passé."

July laughed. "Sorry. We can watch it again sometime. I promise I'll stay awake."

Gareth frowned. "You didn't answer my question."

She shook her head. "I had nightmares most of the night. And no, I don't want to talk about them." Please let him understand. It just wasn't going to be possible to describe the emptiness, or explain why it was terrifying.

After another long look, Gareth nodded. "All right. A distraction then. When we're finished with our coffee, why don't we head out to Skyline Drive? I bet the leaves are still gorgeous."

"That sounds...perfect." She gave his hand another squeeze. "Thank you."

7

Gareth waited until July closed the shower door before lowering his head to the kitchen table. He had to be strong, positive. But it was so hard. Despite what he said to anyone who mentioned it, starting a family had been his idea. He'd nudged, hinted, and prodded until July decided it was what she wanted and started trying to convince him. He'd played at dragging his feet because it didn't seem like guys were supposed to be the ones aching for children. But he was.

When July'd shown him the positive test last month it had been all he could do to avoid leaping for joy. Truth be told, he'd been worried about how long it was taking. Sure, he knew averages and blah blah, but he'd thought it would be faster for them. And now? What was he supposed to do now? What would it take for July to realize how much he was grieving too? But there was no point in trying to explain. She'd say he couldn't possibly understand because he hadn't been the one who was pregnant. That was a point, valid to a degree. But he'd loved that baby every bit as much as she had...couldn't she see that? Maybe she'd see that down the road. He took in a shuddering breath and let the tears fall.

The hand on his shoulder made him jump.

"Gar?" July nudged his arm out of the way and slid into his lap. "Oh, sweetie. I didn't even think..."

He shook his head and forced a smile. "You didn't need to. Still don't. I'm okay. Just sad. Disappointed, too."

She leaned her head against his. "I'm sorry."

He drew his eyebrows together. What was she sorry for? "There's nothing for you to be sorry about."

"We don't know that...maybe I did something wrong. Too much walking or not enough or..."

"Don't. You can't think that way." He pushed his own feelings aside and met her gaze. "We have to trust that there's a reason for this. I did a little reading last night."

"Of course you did."

He smiled. That was more like her. He stuck out his tongue. "If you'll let me finish...it's not uncommon for a first pregnancy to miscarry. I know that doesn't make this any easier, that wasn't what I was trying to say. It doesn't mean something's wrong, necessarily. It just happens, I guess."

July sighed. "That doesn't actually make me feel any better. I want a reason. I want to know what I did, or didn't do. I want some kind of guarantee that it won't happen again."

"I know. I want that too. But..." Gareth shrugged. There weren't any guarantees like that to offer, and statistics and probabilities would make her angry. "We have to trust God."

"I know. I do." She stood and tugged her robe tighter. "Shower's all yours if you're still up for that drive."

"Isn't that Toby?" Gareth nodded across the crowded foyer at a man who looked like his brother-in-law. He didn't see June, but that didn't necessarily rule them out. "I thought they were going to a church with a Saturday service?"

"Sure looks like him. Let's go see. June didn't say anything about them being back here. But I'm not actually sure she knew we were thinking about coming back here. I know there are churches in Bethesda, or heck, other towns in Maryland, that are closer and just as good. But..."

Laughing, Gareth steered them through the crowd, stopping behind Toby. "Boo."

Toby started and spun. "Gareth. Hey man." He stuck out his hand. "Good to see you two. What brings you down this way?"

"Nothing really compares, you know?" Gareth shrugged. "So it's either a church that never seems to feel like home or an insane commute to one that does. I think we're going to be opting for the commute."

"June's going to be glad. We started back last week ourselves, but you're right. It feels like home. Ginger and her husband still go here as well."

"The Three Muskettes, back together again."

July poked Gareth's arm. "That was a lame nickname back then. It's still lame. Why can't we be The Three Musketeers? Girls can be Musketeers, you know."

Gareth shrugged as Toby laughed.

"Ah, here comes June. Want to sit with us for the service? Or were you heading to a small group?"

"July?" June squealed and hurried through the crowd, throwing her arms around her sister.

July returned the hug and grinned. It was her first genuine grin since Friday afternoon and it warmed Gareth's heart. Say what you would about twins, and he had a lot he could say, they had an undeniable bond. It was why he hadn't fought hard when July suggested coming back to church here. Even if June and Toby hadn't already come back, it wouldn't take much to persuade them to. July needed that right now. Frankly, so did he.

"Come on, let's go get seats." June slipped her hand in July's and tugged.

July shot an imploring look at Gareth over her shoulder. He nodded. He was used to tagging along with Toby and June. Liked it, even. And right now, the solid companionship was as much a balm to him as he expected it was for Jules.

GARETH SANK into the couch and propped his feet on the huge ottoman that was not only a footstool, but a coffee table and storage. The thing was enormous and drove him crazy most of the time. But he had to admit that it made a good place for his feet. June had tried to talk them into attending the new small group that she and Toby liked. Thankfully, July wasn't feeling up to it. He hadn't been either, but it seemed like everyone expected him to be all right. It was only July who got asked how she was. Which was fine. It was. She was certainly the one with the physical discomfort, though she said the cramping had stopped and it was more like a normal cycle now. That was probably good. And it was all the analysis he was going to do. What man over the age of fourteen didn't know all about the biology of the female reproductive system? But that didn't mean he wanted to think about it.

Still, it was good she'd begged off so he didn't have to. June and Toby had made noises about skipping and hanging out, but that had tapered off as well. Now July was upstairs tucked into bed for a nap and he had sole control of the TV remote. There was probably a football game on. Nah. He'd look up all the scores and highlights before bed like usual. Then he could talk intelligently at work without actually having to watch. Flipping channels, he found a re-run of *This Old House*. That sounded like just the thing. He'd turned the volume down so he'd be sure not to disturb July and settled in for some vegging time when the phone rang.

With a sigh, he hit mute and answered. "Hello?"

"Hey, it's Toby."

"What's up?" Gareth watched as Norm and his crew pulled down sheets of drywall, exposing uninsulated walls and wiring that looked ancient even to his untrained eye. The camera cut to a shot of snow falling outside. Didn't they ever film this show when it was summer?

"I wanted to see how you were doing. It occurred to me that I hadn't asked."

Gareth let out a short laugh. "Your mind reading's a little slow. I just finished my pity party."

"And I missed it? Was there cake?"

"Ha ha. Though...there might be some cake in the fridge now you mention it...and that would go really well with an afternoon of *This Old House* re-runs." Since the show had switched to a commercial, Gareth stood and ambled into the kitchen.

"Seriously. You okay?"

"Not really. I wanted this baby too, you know? I know I played it off like it was all July's idea...but it wasn't only hers. And it doesn't seem like I'm allowed to be sad our baby's gone." Gareth moved some containers out of the way. Bingo. One last slice. He grabbed the cling-wrap-covered plate and the milk carton. Didn't feel like there was all that much in it, so he'd drink it straight from the container and save on dishes. He added a fork to the pile and made his way back to the living room.

"I think most people assume men don't care until the baby's out and about. Or at least that's what June said."

"Wait. June said people assume it, or June said that men

don't care?" He plopped back onto the couch and began unwrapping the cake.

"She might have made the 'men don't care 'til the baby's crying' comment." Toby cleared his throat. "Which might have been what prompted my call."

Gareth chuckled. "That sounds more like the June I know and love. July too, for that matter."

"So, seeing as how I can imagine how I'd feel if the situation were reversed...I thought I'd give you a call and say I'm sorry. And you know if you need anything blah blah."

"Right up to the 'blah blah' I thought we might have a moment, Tobe." He shook his head, a smile tugging at his lips. "Surprisingly though, that actually helped."

"Well, hey. Points for me then."

"I'll update the spreadsheet later." Gareth forked up a bite of cake and followed it with a swig of milk. "I appreciate the call though. If nothing else, you reminded me we had cake."

Toby laughed. "Go watch your old man home improvement show."

"You know you're going to be surfing channels 'til you find it. Admit it."

"Nuh-uh. There's a game on. Speaking of which, kickoff is soon. Gotta run, this one's gonna make or break my fantasy team."

Gareth shook his head as he hung up the phone. He could watch football and even enjoy it a little. But he wasn't ever likely to be one of those guys who scheduled his weekend around it. And the fantasy team thing? That he absolutely didn't get. He unmuted the TV as Bob came on the screen, rambling about the progress of the renovation. Why did they let him hog so much air time when he did so little of the work?

There ought to be a fantasy remodeling team league. Hmm. That was an idea he could get behind. Surely there were others who'd think it was fun. What would the point system be though? He took another drink and chewed on the possibilities. At least it distracted somewhat from the subtle but constant ache of loss.

8

June checked her watch to confirm the date. She was still late. Her pulse sped up and her eyes flitted to her wrist again. Her co-workers' voices on the mid-week conference call settled into an indistinct, droning buzz. July's miscarriage almost two weeks ago had pushed selfish thoughts of her own possible pregnancy from her mind. But her sister seemed to be doing okay.

Could she really, finally be pregnant? She couldn't wait to tell July. She closed her eyes, a leaden weight settling into the pit of her stomach. Yes she could. Even if it had been almost two full weeks and July was acting normal that didn't mean June's news would be met with joy. Not that she deserved it. Her reaction to July's pregnancy hadn't been stellar. And she hadn't had a legitimate reason like July would.

She dropped her head into her hands. Cart before the horse, anyway. Just because she was late didn't mean she was necessarily pregnant. She'd been late before. Heck, she'd never been particularly regular. June wasn't a clockwork woman like her sister. The thought nagged at her, but she couldn't suppress the flutter of building hope. Two weeks. She'd never been this late before.

Tuning one ear back to her conference call, she pulled up the list of pregnancy symptoms she'd bookmarked and began to run through them. She had enough of them to warrant a quick dash to the drug store at lunch. Maybe this time the test would register.

The sound of her name drew her back to the call. What had they been talking about? She gave herself a firm mental kick before answering the question she hoped they'd asked.

LOCKED IN THE BATHROOM STALL, June stared at the test. Had she done something wrong? She re-read the instructions to be sure. How hard was it to pee on a stick and wait sixty seconds? She swallowed, frowning at the single dark blue line in the window. Maybe she should've bought the one that spelled out the actual word, but they were twice as expensive. Surely with an advanced degree in computers she could handle reading lines in a window.

June held the test up to the light, angling it this way and that as she searched for the slightest trace of the much-desired second line. Nothing. Not even a shadow. She stuffed the test back into the box and pushed the box into the little trash can hanging on the stall wall. She'd wait another couple of days and try again.

She gave the toilet a second flush for the benefit of anyone who might have come in while she was waiting on the test, washed her hands, and went back to her desk. The fluttering in her belly was at war with the heaviness of her heart. She really shouldn't doubt the test. It wasn't the early days of home tests. Still...there was always the chance, right? After all, those things weren't guaranteed. Maybe instead of trying again with the drugstore test, she'd zip in to her doctor for a blood test. Those didn't lie. It was possible she was one of the people who didn't generate enough of the right hormone for the test to work. Wasn't it?

A quick call to the doctor determined she could drop in on her way home from work. They didn't need an appointment for a blood draw. The receptionist, at least, sounded cheery and positive. But then, she always did. June forced her thoughts away from the taunting single line now residing in the trash and studied the malfunctioning code on her screen. This, at least, she could fix.

JUNE DIDN'T RECOGNIZE the number on her cell phone's display. She sent it to voice mail and frowned at her computer. She'd only been in the office for two hours and she was ready to walk out. Why did she possibly need to meet with her supervisor and a representative from HR? No clue...but there was a meeting scheduled in fifteen minutes. Why hadn't she gotten a head's up email from someone?

Heavy butterflies swirled in her stomach. She hadn't broken any policies, her clients were satisfied with her, and so was Bob. Wouldn't there have been rumors if there were layoffs coming? She hadn't heard anything...so what was going on? Meetings with HR on Fridays were never a good thing. The voice mail indicator chimed. Apparently the mystery caller had left a message. June hit play. More than likely it was letting her know that the factory warranty on something she didn't actually own was about to expire. Those annoying calls had been ramping up recently. But she might as well get rid of the message before heading to her mystery meeting.

Hi, June. This is Gina from Dr. Strong's office. Your blood test came back and it's negative. We're sending a prescription over to your preferred pharmacy. If you haven't started your cycle by Monday, go ahead and take that to get things going again. If you have any questions, give us a call back. Have a great weekend.

Oh sure, that was likely. June hit delete and tossed her phone onto her desk. The tests weren't wrong. How was it possible to be so late and not be pregnant? Sure, she'd never been robotic, but things had always been somewhat predictable. The first few months off the pill had been just as regular as when she'd been on it...why the change?

She pushed back from her desk and crossed to the window. Resting her forehead on the cold glass, she angled so she could see down the street and catch a glimpse of the Washington Monument. With most of the leaves off the trees, it was a tad easier to see the spear rising into the sky. But even in the spring and summer simply knowing it was there lifted her spirits. Today it failed to work its magic. If confirmation of her continued un-pregnant state wasn't enough, now she had this meeting downstairs. HR. She hadn't dealt with anyone in HR since filling out her initial paperwork when she was hired four years ago. What was happening?

She wasn't going to solve the mystery by looking out her window. She gathered a notepad and pen, locked her computer, set her phone to vibrate, and dropped it into her pocket. Bob was waiting at the elevator.

She offered him a smile. "Any idea what this is about?"

Bob frowned as he turned to her but gave a short shake of his head. "I'm not allowed to warn you."

June knit her brows. What did that mean? She shot him a questioning glance as the elevator dinged and the doors slid open.

Bob gave another shake of his head and gestured for her to go in. He followed and pushed the button for the fourth floor where HR lived. "I will let you know that I objected to the way they're dealing with this." He gave a shrug. "But it's out of my hands."

The sinking sensation intensified at his words. Was she being fired? For what?

The elevator doors slid open and June stepped out, heading across the small foyer to the main doors. She swiped her badge, only marginally aware of Bob following her, and turned toward the small conference room, stopping short right inside the door.

The room was consumed by a table two sizes too big for the space. High-backed leather chairs were crammed around it. Anthony sat, smirking, at the far end. A vaguely familiar woman sat next to him. Bob pulled out the chair closest to the door and sat, folding his arms over his chest. Not wanting to add to the palpable tension, June chose a seat toward the middle and rested her hands on the table.

"Now that we're all here, we can go ahead and get started. I don't know if you remember me. I'm Paula Johnson, one of the HR Managers for our branch. I assume, Ms. Crawford, that you're familiar with Mr. Wong?"

June gave a slight nod. Of course she was familiar with him. She'd had the typical morning stand-up meeting with him, and the rest of her team, ninety minutes ago. What was going on? She shot a glance toward Bob, trying to gauge his reaction. He sat, arms crossed, with the closest thing to a scowl on his face she'd ever seen. That couldn't possibly be good.

Paula offered a tight smile. "Mr. Wong feels that he's being discriminated against because of his gender and age."

The breath whooshed out of her lungs and she struggled to draw in more as she grappled with the words. Discriminated against? "What? That's..." she stopped herself before finishing the statement with 'insane,' "...incredibly untrue."

She fought the urge to cross her arms, weaving her fingers together on top of her notebook instead. She looked at Anthony. "And I'd really like to know why, Anthony, if you had a problem you didn't come to me as your team leader or to Bob as your Director."

"I'd appreciate it if you'd address your comments to me. Mr. Wong is uncomfortable with you communicating directly with him, for fear that you will continue your harassment and harsh treatment. As for discussing the problem with you, he states that he did so on several occasions." Paula slid a tiny stack of paper down the table. "These are emails that he sent to you, along with your replies."

June took the papers and frowned. She remembered the conversation, but there was nothing about it that was discriminatory. Plus it all took place before she was his supervisor, when they were both equal team members trying to get the demo ready under deadline.

"I'm not sure what in here is supposed to be harassment or discrimination. I asked him if he was planning on fixing his code. He said no, his code was fine. But it wasn't fine, the demo didn't work. So since he was unwilling to fix the problem, I did. Then, when the demo was working perfectly and we were due to meet the client in less than an hour, he rolled back the code to the previous, non-functional version. When this crashed, spectacularly I might add, in front of the client, I had to scramble to get the changes reinstated before we lost all hope of the contract and future business with the client." June pushed the papers back down the table.

"Mr. Wong insists that his code was fine. He also indicates that this is a pattern with you. That you single out his code to modify and then claim that all successes are yours alone, without any acknowledgement of his contributions."

June swiveled to look at Bob. "Bob? You saw the demo, and you saw the code. In fact, you're the one who tasked me with fixing that code because you indicated that Anthony wasn't willing to make any more changes."

Bob nodded. "That's true. And I tried to explain that

already to Ms. Johnson. I also explained that this particular instance occurred prior to your promotion to team lead over Anthony. In addition, I provided several of Anthony's performance reviews that show a trend of unwillingness to fix his products when they're determined to be the cause of integration problems. That is, in fact, why he was transferred to my Directorate from his previous position within the company."

Paula held up a hand. "Those performance reviews are confidential and shouldn't be discussed with Ms. Crawford in the room. Besides, they're irrelevant to the conversation at hand."

"How are they irrelevant? Anthony's trying to show a trend of misconduct from June. I think it's only reasonable that June be allowed to show a trend of insubordination and poor performance on his part. If he'd do his job, and do it right, she wouldn't have to fix his code as often as she does. Does she spend as much time fixing the other members of her team's code? No. But that's simply because she's able to point out the errors—or they find them on their own—and they make the necessary changes. Which is the way a software team is supposed to work." Bob's hand smacked down on the table with a reverberating boom.

June blinked. She'd never seen Bob so worked up. It was good to have him in her corner, and she'd do her best to never get on his bad side.

"I do correct the code of the other team members when needed. Sometimes they even ask for my help when they've hit a wall and can't figure out how to get through it. I know I've made the same offer to you, Anthony." June slid her phone out of her pocket and scrolled through her email. "Here," she tapped in Paula's email address and hit the send button, "that's a forwarded conversation where I offered to sit with him and work through the fixes. He turned me down, insisting his code was fine. Then Doug ran into integration problems with Anthony's code and made a similar offer, copying me as team lead. Anthony turned that down as well, insisting that the problems were not his. No one's code is as perfect as Anthony claims his always is."

"See?" Anthony pointed at June, a scowl on his face. "That's the attitude she always has with me. Condescending. Hostile."

June took a deep breath. Blood pounded in her ears and tiny spots were starting to dance in the corners of her eyes. She couldn't afford to explode, no matter how much she wanted to. She would not scream. "I suppose that's a matter of interpretation. I consider the way you speak to me and everyone else on the team to be essentially the same. And I've told you that. Did you share those email conversations with Ms. Johnson, or shall I? Shall I include the conversations you and I have had with Bob where he's counseled you about learning to work as a member of the team?"

Bob cleared his throat. "Ms. Johnson has those emails and the post-meeting summaries that you both signed. They were provided at the beginning of this farce."

"We have to take all complaints of harassment seriously. And I still see no evidence that Mr. Wong is not being harassed and discriminated against. Even if his work and attitude are sub-par, the tone with which you're addressing him in this meeting is less than professional. I can only presume that when a member of HR is not present you don't bother to attempt to veil your contempt."

"What contempt?" June pressed her fingers into her eyes. This was ridiculous. "I don't have any feelings about Anthony. He's a member of my team who I have unsuccessfully tried to mentor and encourage to collaborate with myself and the rest of his team. In light of his apparent disinterest in being a team player, particularly since I took the position of team lead almost two months ago, I've assigned him projects that are individual and require less integration."

"And in so doing, you set him up for failure." Paula arched her perfectly penciled brow. "Isn't that true? If he's no longer creating code that others have to help test, then any failures rest solely on his shoulders."

"Well, yeah. But that's what he wants, isn't it? He says his code is always fine and that I change it to spite him during integration tests. If he's not part of the larger integration process, then I do less modification and his code stands or fails on its own. If it's perfect, as he says it is, then I don't see why he has a problem." June swallowed a diatribe about not being able to have things both ways. It wouldn't pay to lose her cool any more than she already had.

Bob slammed both his hands on the table and stood. "This is crazy. Anthony, if you're unhappy with your current position, I'll be happy to provide a verification of employment to your next employer. If you aren't interested in switching jobs, then I'm placing you on probation as it is within my purview to do. You will either learn to be a productive member of the team, meaning that you collaborate on your code and accept help as needed, or you will find another place of employment. And you need to make that decision quickly."

Paula pushed to her feet and leaned forward on the conference table. "You may be within your rights to penalize Mr. Wong in this manner, however I will be instigating a full investigation of Ms. Crawford. If I find even the slightest whiff of harassment and discrimination from another employee, she'll be summarily dismissed." She turned and leveled her gaze at June. "Don't think that having Bob in your corner will always protect you. We're an equal opportunity employer, which means we look out for our minorities when they run up against people like you."

"You can look all you want, Paula. June's one of the best employees I've had the privilege of working with. You won't find anything." Bob turned to June. "Come on. You've got work you should be doing. As do I."

Willing her shaking legs to hold her, June scooted away from the table. She gathered her notebook, shot a confused frown at Anthony, and followed Bob from the room. Why had Anthony gone straight to HR? Was she so hard to talk to?

Bob gave her shoulder an awkward pat as they waited for the elevator. "Welcome to management. There's always going to be someone like that. Someone who wants to get ahead without doing the work or putting in the time. You've got to learn to weather the storm."

"Does it get easier?"

Bob shook his head. "Nope. You keep doing your job the way you have been. Stick to your ethics, treat people right, and this'll blow over. With any luck, you'll end up with someone who's actually useful on your team."

Did he mean a reformed, productive Anthony or a replacement? Did she care? If this was how management worked, maybe she wasn't cut out for it.

9

June stretched and flopped over onto her stomach, tugging the blankets tighter around her shoulders. Toby had gotten up a little while ago, but Saturday mornings were for lazing in bed. Maybe he'd bring her some coffee and she could wallow here even longer. Last night she'd managed to avoid telling Toby about the negative pregnancy test and her meeting with Paula by feigning illness and heading straight to bed when she got home from work. It wasn't completely a sham. Every time the events of the day replayed in her mind, nausea roiled in her gut. Couldn't she do anything right?

The side of the bed sank as Toby settled on the edge next to her. "Morning, sleepyhead. I brought you coffee."

June wriggled to a sitting position and smiled as she reached for the steaming mug in his hand. "Mind reader."

He chuckled and held the drink out of reach. "I heard your mental call for caffeine from downstairs and am holding it hostage 'til you tell me what's wrong."

Her shoulders slumped. Why had she thought she could

fool him? He always knew. "All right. But I want coffee while I tell you."

Lips pursed, Toby nodded. "Fair enough. But I'm wrestling it out of your hands if you try to skimp on details." His tone softened. "You worried me last night."

Of course she had. She hadn't meant to, but she'd needed a little time to push it aside. Or immerse herself in her misery before having her concerns dismissed. He'd be sympathetic, to a point. But Toby was a fixer and she hadn't been ready for that. She still wasn't, but her time had run out. After taking a bracing sip of coffee, June related the details of the meeting.

"That's the most ridiculous thing I've ever heard." Toby scowled. "What a little...at least Bob had your back. And he's right, to some degree. That is kind of how management works. Most of the time you can just do your job, but there will always be situations where you have to deal with idiots. And bureaucracy. And bureaucratic idiots."

June snickered. "I get that. But if doing my job, with a focus on making our stuff work and our clients happy, gets me hauled down to HR and charged with harassment and discrimination, I don't know if I'm cut out for management. Maybe I stink at leadership. Shouldn't I have been able to...I don't know, convince him somehow to work with me or one of the others on our team? If I was good at leading, wouldn't people want to follow me?"

"You can't take it personally. This guy's been driving you nuts since he started, long before you were in charge of getting him to perform. It's not you."

"How am I supposed to take it if not personally? He questioned my integrity to the point that now HR is questioning my integrity. Clearly there's something wrong with me."

Toby rubbed her leg. "There's nothing wrong with you."

"Whatever. I can't lead a team and I can't get pregnant. I'm useless at home and at work. Why do you even stay?"

"Don't say that. I love you and there's nowhere else I want to be. If you don't want to be a team lead, why don't you step back down? They can find someone else and you can focus on doing the work that you enjoy. Then Anthony'll be out of your hair—you can refuse to deal with him. And the baby thing...we've got lots of time yet. There's no point in worrying about it. It'll happen when God wants it to happen." Toby leaned over and pressed a kiss to her forehead. "Finish your coffee and jump in the shower and we'll go do something to get your mind off things."

Over the top of her mug, June watched him as he ambled from the room. Nothing to worry about. Right. She could just imagine how well it'd go over for her to step back from her new promotion. Bob would be disappointed in her. Anthony triumphant. The rest of her team confused. And it would simply solidify her own failure and inability. There was no stepping back. She might have to switch jobs if things got worse—and if she did that, she could make sure to find a position that wasn't managerial. She closed her eyes as her stomach twisted. She didn't want to find a new job, she loved where she was and most of the people she worked with. Even if she was a miserable failure when it came to management, she'd stick it out. Besides, if she wasn't going to have kids, she might as well have some kind of career. Even if she wasn't particularly good at it.

She drained the last of the coffee from her mug and threw her legs over the side of the bed. She'd get up and shower and let Toby drag her out of the house. It wouldn't help in the long term, but it might help for today. Why couldn't he admit that it was okay to start to worry, at least a little, about not being pregnant? Didn't he want children? He'd said he did...was he just humoring her?

$\sim$

"YOU WANNA GO to small group with us?" June turned to July as the postlude started and people began filing out of the sanctuary.

July looked at Gareth who shrugged.

"Come on, you'll like it. And I'll like knowing someone." June grinned. It was good to have her sister at the same church again. It was long drive for them, but they seemed okay with it, so June was going to take advantage.

"All right, all right." July laughed, gathering her things. "Might as well. We were thinking of looking at the various classes and seeing if there was one that interested us."

"Look no further. Seriously." June thumped her sister on the shoulder with her finger. "I want you two to come with us." Out of the corner of her eye she saw Toby roll his eyes. "I saw that."

"What?" Toby put on his best look of wounded innocence.

June shook her head. "I thought you were on my side. Weren't you saying in the car that you hoped they'd join us?"

"Yeah. But I was going to be more subtle about the whole thing."

Gareth chuckled. "You? Subtle? I'd like to see that. You and June are perfect for each other if only because you both go barreling in, guns a'blazing."

As they made their way through the church to the small group room, June's thoughts whirled. Was that how she came across? June forced the corners of her mouth up as everyone continued poking fun, but her heart sank. No wonder her team hated her and wanted her out. Did Bob agree with them? Was he serious about his stick-to-it advice? Was he secretly looking for a replacement, someone who wasn't so brazenly opinionated?

"June. July." Ginger squealed and hurried across the room, throwing her arms around them. "You're both here. This is awesome."

"The gang's back together again." July winked and pulled Gareth closer.

"Come sit over here, plenty of room with us." Ginger pointed to a group of chairs clustered on the far side of the room.

As they got settled, further conversation was put on hold when Kevin called for quiet and opened the class in prayer. They were starting a study of James this week, and the discussion kept things focused primarily on the first four verses. June struggled to relate to someone who could consider suffering joy. Sure, suffering for the faith, maybe. Then there's a higher purpose, a reason behind it. But how could failing as a manager and as a woman possibly contribute to the perfecting of her faith? It was all so irrelevant. She looked around the room. Everyone seemed so involved, so encouraged by the idea. Obviously they had no idea what real suffering was. July caught her eye and June flinched. Okay, not everyone. July understood. Probably better than June. Surely it was worse to lose a baby than to not be able to make one in the first place. But why did July look like she was enjoying the lesson?

At the end of class, they went around the room sharing prayer requests. No one was taking notes. Did anyone actually pray during the week? June dug out an old bulletin and began to scribble down the requests. That was at least something she could do. Maybe praying for other people would help her focus less on her own problems. Laura had a stomach virus she couldn't seem to shake—that had to be hard with two kids and a job. A few mentions of work troubles. June could identify with that. The woman next to Ginger shook her head.

Ginger glanced at Martin, at his nod she took a deep breath. "We're expecting. We just started trying, kind of see what happens, you know? And it worked right off. We'll have a baby around the middle of July."

The class erupted with congratulations. June's smile stiffened as her heart sank into her shoes and a buzz gnawed at her ears. Was everyone but her going to get pregnant? She jolted when July's elbow connected with her ribs.

"Oh. Um. Nothing. We're good." She caught the confused and semi-concerned look Toby shot her as the class continued around the circle. Did he want her to share now? Hadn't he said there was nothing to worry about? With Ginger's news and July clearly being able to conceive without too much trouble, June wasn't going to let anyone else in on her fear that she was irreparably broken. Particularly when Toby'd made it clear that he disagreed and they only needed to be patient.

After Kevin closed the class in prayer, little groups of conversation formed as people discussed lunch plans and the coming week. Ginger and Martin hurried off for another family gathering, sparing June the ordeal of faking an appropriate amount of glee. She'd have to drum up the giddiness at some point, of course, but maybe by then it wouldn't be completely forced.

"So...you talk to Mom and Dad lately?" July tucked her hands in her pockets. Behind her, Gareth mimed hanging himself.

June snickered and shook her head. "Why?"

July glanced over her shoulder and rolled her eyes. "They're coming down for Thanksgiving. Surprise."

"But...they...it's..."

"Exactly." July handed her Bible to Gareth. "So whose turn is it to host and cook?"

July groaned. "We agreed that we'd all have our own little family celebrations this year. There would be no huge gathering. Doesn't she remember this conversation? She was excited not to have to travel and Dad was looking forward to some restaurant in downtown Chicago that had...what was it?"

"Ostrich instead of turkey. I know." July stared at her toes, her voice nearly inaudible. "I think it's because of the baby.

They're worried, and no matter what I said they simply refuse to believe I'm okay." She glanced up, meeting June's eyes. "And I am. I'm not thrilled, obviously, but at least it means we can get pregnant. We'll just wait a month and try again."

Pain stabbed through June's heart. July hadn't meant it like that. Of course she hadn't. "If that's the reason, then I think it's your turn to cook and host."

July's eyebrows lifted and June grimaced. It had come out nastier than she'd intended. Not that she hadn't intended some of the nasty, just not that much.

"Fine. I'll let you know the details when they're figured out. If you want to come, we'd love to have you." July spun on her heel and grabbed Gareth's arm, pulling him away from a conversation with Toby and Laura's husband Matthew.

"July. Wait." June sighed and crossed to her sister. "You know that's not what I meant."

"Do I? You haven't exactly been supportive. Or sympathetic."

"Oh, of course, it's all about you. Did you even once think about why? You *lied* to me, Jules. Not hid something, outright lied. And then, without any concern for the fact that we're having no success, you just jam yours in my face and expect me to drop everything and jump around for joy. And I should have, I get that. But I might've been better equipped to do that if you hadn't set it up so it came across like it took you all of a week to end up pregnant. I'm coming up on four months of trying and all I have to show for it is forty-five extra pounds and a closet full of clothes that don't fit." June glanced around the not-quite empty room and heat flooded her cheeks. Great. She hadn't wanted to share during prayer time, and now she'd blabbed anyway. No one was staring, but surely they'd all heard.

"The weight gain started before you went off the pill, but the rest of that is fair. I guess. But what's your excuse now? The baby's gone, so we're both back to square one."

"No we aren't." June kept her voice low. "You said it yourself. At least you know you can get pregnant. All I know is that my system is getting more out of whack with each passing day, and if I have another month where I gain ten pounds while counting every calorie that goes into my mouth...I'm not going to be able to take it."

July opened her mouth but Gareth held up his hand.

"Maybe we should table this discussion until later?" Gareth slipped his arm around July's waist. "We're happy to host Thanksgiving if that's what you want. Will you help with the food?"

"Tell me what you want me to bring."

"We'll do that." Gareth spoke before July could interject. "Come on, let's get home and get some lunch."

June slumped into a chair as she watched them leave. Toby was still talking to Matthew. At least the two of them had hit it off.

"Hey." Laura perched on the edge of the chair next to June and offered a sympathetic smile. "I couldn't help overhearing..."

June scrubbed her hands over her face. "You and everyone in the building. Sorry."

"It's all right. Can I pry a little?"

"Why not? I've made my failure public knowledge, you might as well have the details."

Laura frowned. "You're not a failure. Don't give up hope. It took Matt and me nine months to get pregnant the first time. You can drive yourself crazy if you focus on averages and all that. But after four-ish months of trying, which sounds like about where you are..."

June nodded.

"I found a great book. It goes through all the biology, stuff you think you learned in school but there's so much that never got covered. Then it does a thorough job showing you how to chart your cycles to get a handle on when you're fertile and so on and so forth...it's a great resource. If you give me your email address, I'll send you the title when I get home."

"That'd be great. I've browsed online but...it's overwhelming. There are so many books out there and I don't really want to spend a fortune or start a library." June rattled off her email.

Laura chuckled as she typed June's email into her phone then read it back. "I'll get that to you today. For now, I should run and save the nursery workers' sanity."

10

July ground her teeth together the whole way home. Where did June get off acting like that? Fine. Maybe June had a few good points. She and Gareth shouldn't have kept it a secret, or at least not for so long. But she'd gotten in the habit of not mentioning it, and then when she'd suspected she was pregnant...well, she'd had to tell June they were trying. She couldn't drop a pregnancy out of the blue, that would've crushed her sister. No matter what June thought, that wasn't something July was trying to do.

"I can hear your wheels spinning all the way over here." Gareth pulled into the driveway and shut off the car. "Care to share?"

July sighed. "I hate fighting with June."

"Then don't."

"Oh sure. Cause it's that easy." July punched her seatbelt release and pushed open the car door.

"It is, though. Just don't engage." Gareth gathered their church bag from the back seat. "She'll get the hint eventually."

July turned, hand on the knob of the carport door. "The

thing is, she has some valid points. I handled this whole thing badly. In a lot of ways, I set it up to fail."

"We handled it badly. Not telling the world was my idea, at least more so than yours." He shrugged. "I'm still not convinced it was a mistake. Next time...well next time I don't think we should tell anyone until after we've been to the doctor, maybe not until you're through the first trimester."

"Really?" July dropped her purse on the kitchen counter. "You're that worried about it happening again? The doctor said it wasn't likely...that these things sometimes happen."

"I know, but it was hard to untell people. As great as it was to have people congratulating us and sharing our excitement for the baby, I think next time we're better off waiting."

"Hmm. We'll see."

"Jules..."

"What? I don't think we have to decide right this minute. Let's wait until I get pregnant again, okay?"

"Yeah, okay. Hey, did you get any more details from your sister about the issue with her job? Toby filled me in some, but I didn't make him explain the whole thing, figured you could catch me up."

July frowned. What job thing? She shook her head. "June never said anything to me about work...what's going on?"

Gareth raised his eyebrows. "She didn't say anything?"

"No...but she's been distant for a few weeks. Getting anything other than cheerful and breezy has been a challenge." July dropped into a recliner and leaned back. She kicked off her shoes and sighed. "So fill me in."

Gareth related the meager details he had. July pursed her lips. Her sister had to be incredibly upset with her not to have mentioned at least some of this. It sounded like June was worried she was on the edge of being fired...and she still hadn't wanted to say something to July? It was as if a piece of her heart ripped off. She closed her eyes. She'd done effectively the same thing to June...but about something that mattered even more than a work issue.

"I need to go call her."

He checked his watch. "I doubt they're back yet. Toby was going to try and get her to go out to eat, thought it might cheer her up. Plus I thought you were fighting. Doesn't that usually last longer?"

July waived away his concern. "I owe her an apology. Maybe two of them." Seeing Gareth's quizzical expression she sighed. "Look, if I'm this hurt by her not telling me about a work situation it means she was perfectly justified in her reaction to everything surrounding the baby. She's my twin. It didn't sit right, but I'd thought it might be nice to have something that was only mine."

"And you enjoyed it."

"You're right, I did...but that's because I didn't think it through very well. Now that the shoe's on the other foot?" July shook her head. She wasn't going to explain any more. He'd either get it or not. Either way, she was done keeping secrets from her sister.

Gareth gave her a long look before shrugging. "I'm going to go fix some sandwiches for lunch. Should be ready when you're finished with your call."

~

"Thought I might find you here." July pulled out a chair and sat at her sister's table in the crowded sandwich shop.

"What do you want, Jules?" June dropped her sandwich back onto the paper bag it came in and crossed her arms.

"I tried to call you all afternoon yesterday." July caught her lower lip with her teeth. "Look, I'm sorry. About all of it."

June lifted an eyebrow.

Of course she wasn't going to make it easy. When had she

ever? July sighed. "Toby mentioned the work thing to Gar, who asked me for details and...I didn't like how that shoe fits on the other foot."

June picked up her sandwich.

"Okay. Well...I guess I'll let you get back to your lunch." July scooted away from the table and stood, hunching her shoulders. "Mom and Dad will be here on Wednesday. Will you meet us for dinner?"

"Instead of Thursday?"

July shook her head. "Course not."

"I'll ask Toby."

July closed her eyes. She'd beg if she had to, though it was unlikely to matter. "June...please?"

"All right. Fine. We'll come to dinner on Wednesday, too." June frowned.

"Yay." July pulled the chair back out and sat. "Thank you. So...are you going to tell me about this creep at work? Do you want me to come back with you? I'd bet together we can take him."

June snickered. "We probably could, but I don't think that's going to help my case any."

As June filled July in on the details of her meeting with HR, July's blood began to boil. By the time June finished, July could barely sputter. "But...that's...what?"

"Pretty much." June took a huge bite of her sandwich, deftly catching a drip with her thumb. "But I don't see what I can do about it. Bob says play along and copy him on any emails. And I'm not having any in-person conversations with the guy. If he comes by my office to ask a question, I make him wait 'til the rest of the team is present or Bob can swing by. Mostly he's stopped coming by."

"Smart girl."

June lifted a shoulder. "Only somewhat. Bob said there's already been another complaint because of it. Something about me not treating him fairly because I make other people be present when he has questions. He feels it's my attempt to shame and degrade him."

"Oh good grief."

"I told Bob the only way I was going to have a private communication with him was via email, because at least then there was a paper trail. Bob passed that along to HR and, so far, they understand that at some level I have to be allowed to protect myself. But I'm not making any friends on that side of the house."

"But your boss, Bob, he's still okay, right?"

June nodded.

"You should be fine then. And who knows, maybe once this guy realizes he can't get away with his behavior, he'll decide to leave and save everyone the hassle."

"That'd be nice...but I'm not counting on it. There's already been some damage to my reputation. His HR friend has stirred up the upper management and Bob's had to do some serious damage control. I'm not convinced they won't make me a scape goat in order to avoid a lawsuit." June checked the time on her phone and stood. "I have to run. I'm glad you came and found me...I don't like fighting with you, Jules."

July stood and pulled her sister into a tight hug. "Me either."

June wove through the packed tables on her way out. July sighed. Something was still off. June seemed...reserved. Like she was hiding something. Not that she didn't have every right to do so, of course. But they'd never had secrets growing up. And as much as she hadn't minded keeping a secret of her own, being on the other side of things stank. She shoved her hands into her pockets and headed back to work. At least you always knew where you stood with numbers.

~

JULY PULLED into the carport and frowned in the rearview mirror at the car parked on the street in front of their house. There was a tacit agreement among the neighbors that guests would park in front of the house they were visiting, or in the respective driveways. Since the old streets were narrower than those in newer subdivisions, it helped keep the road easier to navigate. She wasn't expecting anyone today...so who was parked there?

Sitting here wasn't going to figure it out. She grabbed her computer and purse and shoved open the car door. Maybe she'd leave it for Gareth to figure out. She didn't have the energy. She had at least thirty minutes before he got home, and she fully intended to put those minutes to good use snuggled under a quilt on the living room couch. She might put something mindless on the television. Or she might just admit that she wanted to nap. With a jaw-stretching yawn, July unlocked the door and trudged into the kitchen. She dropped her things by the door and reached down to unzip the calf-length boots she'd worn. Purchasing them had been a moment of insanity, but now that they lived in her closet she forced herself to suffer through a day in them at least once every other month.

"Hi, sweetie."

July flailed her arms to keep from falling over and stood, breathless. "Mom? I thought you weren't coming 'til Wednesday...how'd you get in?"

Betty smiled. "I arranged it with Gareth. He left a key in the carport for us."

July scowled. She hated having a key where someone could stumble across it. Gareth knew that.

"Don't worry, dear. It's on the counter and your house is no worse for wear."

"Sorry." July forced the corners of her mouth up as she crossed the nap off her afternoon activities. What was she going to make for dinner? Bracing her hand on the wall, she leaned over and unzipped the other boot as she flipped through her mental inventory of the freezer. It was going to have to be spaghetti. "Let me run my boots upstairs and change. You and Dad settled in the guest room okay?"

"Everything's lovely. Don't rush." Betty leaned back, a look of scrutiny on her face. "You look tired."

"I'm fine. I'll be right back." July brushed a kiss across her mother's cheek and hurried upstairs. If she looked tired it was because she *was* tired. Which was why she'd tried so hard to limit her parents' visit to two days. Now they'd be here five. Unless Gareth had already let them extend beyond that. She tossed her shoes into the closet and gently banged her head against the door. She was going to kill him.

Rather than the pajama pants and sweatshirt she'd been dreaming about on her drive home, July pulled on nice jeans and a sweater. Her dad disliked spaghetti and it was even odds that he'd drag them out to eat once he realized what she was making. Might as well save herself having to change again. Plus then she wouldn't have to listen to her mom's semi-veiled comments about how casual everything had gotten. She dug through her drawer for a pair of thick socks, her one nod to pure comfort and her protesting feet, and padded back downstairs. Gareth had better get home on time.

"There's my girl." Her dad's voice boomed out of the living room as she turned the corner.

"Hi, Dad. How was the trip?"

Ed chuckled and settled back into the deep cushions of the couch. "About as good as air travel can be these days. Seems like they make seats smaller and closer together every time you turn around. Getting so that I'm going to have to save up for first class if I'm going to be flying more than two hours."

July pecked his cheek. "Well, I appreciate you making the trip." Even if they were two days early.

"Blame your mother, not me." His voice was a conspiratorial

whisper and accompanied with a wink. "I tried to talk her out of it, but you know how she is when she gets an idea in her head. Full steam ahead. Easier to batten down the hatches and ride the waves."

July smiled in spite of herself. That was so like her father. But it had been working for him for thirty years, so why change it? "Can you deal with spaghetti? I was planning to hit the grocery store tomorrow."

Ed wrinkled his nose but nodded. "Just this once, and only for you."

"Thanks." July peered around the archway that separated the living room from the kitchen. "Where'd Mom go?"

Ed gave a shrug and picked up his book. "She's somewhere. You know how your mother is."

Stifling a groan, July nodded and trudged into the kitchen. She did know how her mother was. That was the problem. The government could talk about a reasonable expectation of privacy all they wanted, but if they ever wanted to know everything about someone, they just needed to get her mother invited over for dinner some night. Whatever. She had no secrets. Not really.

She pulled a pound of ground beef out of the freezer, unwrapped it, and dropped it into a pan. Cranking the heat, she covered the pan and turned to dig out her pasta pot. Despite her frustration, she smiled as she pulled the heavy stainless steel pot from under the counter. The pasta strainer insert had sold her on the thing, and Gareth had given it to her for Christmas two years ago. It had paid for itself a hundred times over in avoided burns. No matter how hard she tried, she had never mastered pouring boiling water into a strainer without splashing herself at least a little. And she had the tiny scars to prove it.

With the water on the back burner heating up, July lowered the heat on the meat and flipped the frozen block over, scraping the browned meat off and giving it a quick sprinkle of Italian seasoning and garlic salt before digging around in the pantry. Where was the jar of sauce? She'd seen it the other day, hadn't she? By the time the meat was fully cooked and the water was bubbling cheerily, July gave up. There was no sauce. She frowned at the cans of crushed tomatoes, tomato paste, and tomato sauce lined up on the counter. They were the only tomato products in the pantry. It was going to have to do.

She was opening the first can when Gareth came in from the carport.

"Something smells good." He dropped his things by the door and crossed to wrap his arms around her from behind.

"Spaghetti. And I will get my revenge." July pried the lid off of the crushed tomatoes and leaned back to meet his eyes. "You won't know when. You won't know where. But I will get you for this."

Gareth kissed her forehead and released her. "You say it like I had some choice in the whole thing. She called and explained how it was going to be. What was I supposed to do?"

"Say no." July dumped the contents of the can over the meat and pursed her lips as she stirred. Maybe just half of the tomato sauce. But what would she do with the rest of the can?

"Have you met your mother?"

July set the can down with a thunk. "Okay. All right. You're right. But you could've given me a heads up."

Gareth arched a brow.

"She told you not to."

"Ding. And you and I both know you wouldn't have been able to act well enough to fool her."

"Yeah, well. You're still going to pay." July squeezed the handles of the can opener hard enough to send a little drop of tomato sauce spurting out.

He shook his head. "I'm going to go change. I love you."

"Yeah yeah." July shooed him away.

"DID YOU KNOW ABOUT THIS?" July held her cell phone to her ear as she turned the corner. No one had wanted to join her on a quick walk after dinner, so she had twenty blissful minutes to herself.

"Know about what?" June yawned into the phone. "What are you doing, anyway?"

"Going for a walk. It was the only thing I could think of to get out of the house. Mom and Dad are here."

"Thought they weren't coming until Wednesday."

"Exactly." July slowed her pace. "And I don't know if they're still planning to leave Friday or if that's changed too."

June snickered.

"It isn't funny."

"It kinda is. At least for me."

July sighed. "Does that mean you won't help me out?"

"No. But I am going to laugh. What'cha need?"

"Can you take them to dinner tomorrow night?

"Are we still doing dinner together on Wednesday night?"

"If I say no does it change the answer?"

"Maybe." June groaned. "I don't want to see them every day this week."

"Oh, believe me, I get that. Come on, June. Please?" July hated the whine that crept into her voice.

"All right. But you owe me."

July cleared her throat. "I'm going to owe you more."

"Why? What else do you need?"

"Well...I can't come back from a walk and say 'Oh, by the way, you're eating with June and Toby tomorrow.'"

"Why not? They are."

"June."

"Fine. I'll call, act surprised that they're already there, and invite them out. But you're right, you owe me big. Like tickets to the Kennedy Center big."

"Just tell me when. You're the best." July slowed as she rounded the corner. The porch lights gleamed in the distance. "I'll be home in about three minutes. So wait five or ten, then call? I'll figure out a way to make sure Mom answers."

"You're pathetic."

"I know. Believe me, I know." July ended the call and tucked her phone back into her pocket. At least she'd bought an evening to grocery shop for Thanksgiving without her mom peering over her shoulder and second guessing every ingredient. She sighed again and headed up the driveway. She loved her mother. Got along with her, even. She just didn't need to have her under foot, wondering when the miscarriage was going to come up in conversation. That was the real problem, of course. She didn't want to talk about it, and Mom was going to want to talk it to death. Maybe she could mentally gear up for it tomorrow and approach it herself on Wednesday. Whatever happened, July needed to keep it from being a topic of conversation at the dinner table on Thanksgiving. That wasn't fair to June. Or anyone.

11

June double checked that the pies weren't going to slide around in the back seat on their way to July and Gareth's. All things considered, dinner on Tuesday night with her parents hadn't been horrible. It probably helped that it had been fairly quick. They'd met at a restaurant in Arlington near June's office, eaten, and then gone their separate ways. Now she only had to get through the Thanksgiving meal, make her excuses, and she'd have a blissful four-day weekend to forget the insanity at work. And maybe polish up her resume. A knife twisted in her gut. She didn't want to find a new job. But how she was going to survive at her current one?

HR had now demanded that she not single Anthony out by communicating only via email. She'd tried communicating with everyone only by email, but that hadn't flown either. So now she was stuck. She wasn't going to have any in-person conversations with the man if there weren't witnesses present. But he'd made it so she wasn't able to have witnesses around all the time by crying foul when she'd called mini team meetings every time he had a question. Now she wasn't allowed to at even generate a paper trail. What was she supposed to do?

"Hey." Toby put his hands on her shoulders and began to knead her knotted muscles. "No thinking about work on Thanksgiving."

"Who says I'm thinking about work? I could've been thinking about a whole afternoon with my mother and her not-so-veiled comments about my weight."

"You were muttering. So unless you've started calling your mother Anthony..."

June groaned. "No. But I'd like to lock them in a room together and see who comes out alive."

Toby let out a short laugh. "I'd pay to watch that. Still. She was pretty good Tuesday night. Maybe your dad'll keep her in check. Besides, I don't care what anyone says, you're still the most gorgeous woman I know." He pulled her close and kissed her.

Clearly he needed to get out more.

"No, I don't." Toby tapped her nose.

June cocked her head to the side, brows drawn together.

"Need to get out more. I can read you like a book. Even when you're being snarky. Now come on, we should get a move on. It won't pay to be late."

Traffic was slightly better than on a non-holiday, though there were still entirely too many cars on the Beltway. People should know better than to try and drive the I-95 corridor on a holiday. Even waiting for the actual day there was too much local traffic to make it easy on the interstate commuters. June counted twelve state license plates, not including Virginia, Maryland or D.C., on the thirty minute drive to her sister's house.

Betty pulled open the front door as they swung into the driveway and waved. June checked the clock on the dash.

"We're not late. We're not even close to late. Why is she standing by the door already?"

"Maybe July kicked her out of the kitchen and she had nothing else to do."

June chuckled. That could actually happen. "Well let's get in there before she lets all the heat out of the house. It's cold today."

They each grabbed a pie and hurried up the walk. At the door, June took the pecan pie from Toby and slid past her mother with a perfunctory air kiss. "Let me take these in and see what I can do to help Jules." She scurried down the hall before her mother could object.

"Oh thank goodness you're here." July craned her neck, her gaze focused behind June as she spoke. Her voice dropped to a whisper. "She's going to drive me insane."

June slid the pies onto the counter. "You're the one who agreed to them coming."

"Right. Agreed to it." July shook her head and pointed at the oven. "Will you check the turkey? It should be done fairly soon and Mom has me so paranoid about overcooking it that I'm liable to serve it raw."

"Doesn't it have a pop-up thingy?"

"She pulled it out, said they were unreliable and shouldn't be trusted. There's an instant-read thermometer by the stove."

Fighting the urge to roll her eyes, June grabbed the thermometer and some pot holders and opened the oven. The dark-brown turkey skin gleamed and a heavenly aroma wafted out. "Smells good."

She poked the thermometer between the leg and the body and watched the digital readout. "Um…I think it's done."

July squatted beside her and looked in. "Great. Well, it'll have a chance to rest, I guess. They say that's good for it, right?"

"Think so. But you're the Food Network watcher, not me. How do we keep it hot?"

"I'll take care of it. Can you make sure the table's set? I sent Mom in to do it a while ago, but she never came back to say she was finished, so I'm guessing she got distracted."

Chuckling, June crossed into the dining room. The extra leaf in the table meant there was very little room to get by on either end. Still, the deep gold table cloth looked lovely against the bright orange chargers under the gleaming white china. Crystal goblets sparkled by every setting and deep red cloth napkins were twisted artfully into swans in the middle of each plate. A pitcher of water sat on either end of the table and trivets waited to be laden with serving bowls and platters.

"It's all set. Is there something I can start putting out?"

July shook her head. "I think I've got it. Why don't you go find everyone and have them take a seat. By the time everyone finally meanders in, we should be ready."

"SHOULD YOU REALLY EAT THAT, DEAR?" Betty nodded to the skinny slice of pumpkin pie on June's plate. "You can't complain about your weight if you're going to ignore any semblance of healthy eating."

June's stomach clenched and bile worked its way up the back of her throat. She set the pie down on the arm of July's sofa and gave her mother a tight smile.

"So, July, when will you and Gareth be able to get pregnant again? The doctor must have given you some guidelines."

July shot her sister an apologetic glance. "I told you Wednesday, Mom, they don't have any set recommendations anymore. We haven't decided if we'll wait a bit or keep trying."

June looked at her watch. If she wasn't going to be able to eat a tiny slice of pie she wanted to go home. Her mother had commented on every bite she'd taken during dinner and now she seemed determined to talk about the one subject a rational person would avoid.

"What about you, June? Anything to report?"

Her jaw dropped and she bit off the start of a screech.

Toby reached over and squeezed her hand. "Not yet, Mom. But that's still perfectly normal."

Betty nodded. "Oh, of course. Though you'll want to watch your weight. I was reading an article just the other day that talked about how important the health of the mother-to-be was in terms of conception and the reduction of issues during pregnancy. Plus, well, your frame simply can't handle that much weight."

Heat spread up June's neck and singed her cheeks as her teeth ground together. There was no benefit in replying. There wasn't. June focused on her breathing but that made it accelerate. One. Two. Oh forget it. She stood.

"You know what, Mom? I'm well aware of every pound that I've gained since Toby and I started trying to get pregnant. Believe me. And if you bothered to look, or even talk to July or anyone else, you'd know that I hardly eat anything anymore, but the weight keeps piling on."

Her mother sniffed, eyes darting to June's uneaten slice of pie.

"Oh, fine. I was going to have a sliver of pie on Thanksgiving. Sue me." She picked up the pie, her knuckles turning white as she gripped the plate.

"June..." Toby tugged on her sleeve.

She shook him off. "It's not as if you care, Mom. You're only here because July miscarried. Well, bully for her. At least one of your daughters isn't broken and useless."

"I never said you were either of those things." Betty's face was the picture of innocent injury.

"You didn't have to. I'm not blind or stupid. I can still read between the lines even if I don't fit between them anymore."

She stalked into the kitchen and slammed the plate down on the counter. She shouldn't have said those things about July... her sister had every right to pain as she did. But honestly, why couldn't her mother just accept that both of her daughters were hurting? Wasn't it worse in some ways to wonder whether or not you'd ever be able to conceive? At least July had hope.

"Hey." Toby rubbed her shoulder. "You want to go home?"

June turned and buried her face in his shoulder. Her voice was muffled and strained. "Yes. But we'd never hear the end of it."

"Who cares? She'd get over it eventually."

June sighed and leaned back to meet his eyes. "No, she wouldn't. And I'd have to do even more groveling than I'm already in for."

"I don't think you have any groveling to do. If you need to apologize, then so does she."

"Like it works that way." She managed a small smile. "Come on, might as well face the music now. Maybe she'll retreat to her room in a huff and we can make our escape."

June and Toby made their way back to the living room, conversation quieting as they sat.

"Sorry." June met July's gaze with a pained smile.

"Don't worry about it. We understand." July leaned over to pat her knee.

Betty's eyebrows rose. "That's it?"

June closed her eyes and counted to five. "Yes. That's it. I'm sorry. That should be enough."

"Well, it isn't, and I'm surprised your sister is okay with it at all. You need to remember that your inability to have children isn't only about you. All my friends have grandchildren already. Do you have any idea how humiliating it is to not have any of my own? At least July is making some progress, but really, June. Are you even working on it? You seem very laid back about the whole thing."

Toby's eyes narrowed to slits and his pulse jumped in his neck. "Surely in all the reading you're apparently doing you've discovered that being laid back is exactly the right way to be?"

June hadn't seen him this angry in a long time, though she doubted anyone else noticed.

"Of course you don't want to get stressed, but there has to be some bit of urgency. After all, you're not getting any younger." Betty held up her hand when Toby opened his mouth. "That's neither here nor there. The point is that there has to be more you could be doing. If you'd apply yourself I could have a grandchild by this time next year."

Betty stormed from the room.

Did that just happen? Did her mother make her daughter's inability to have children about her? June looked at her dad.

"Sweetie...she's..." Ed frowned. "I don't know what she is. Off base. Really, really off base. I'd offer to talk to her but...you know your mother as well as I do. I do think that, when she's had some time to think about it, she'll realize what she said and be sorry. She'd never hurt you intentionally."

June sighed. She couldn't withstand the pleading look on her dad's face. "I know." She dragged a hand through her hair. "I think we're going to head home."

July stood, arms crossed tightly over her chest. "Want to take any of the food home?"

"Better not. You've got company. And, well, I shouldn't be eating it anyway."

"I'M GOING to go take a bath." June kicked off her shoes and leaned down to pick them up.

"You sure you're okay?" Toby grabbed her hand and pulled her close.

"I'm sure. Go watch your game." June smiled and kissed his

cheek. He didn't watch much football, but he did like to see the games on Thanksgiving. Something about a father-son tradition that he didn't want to break because of geography. "Call your dad."

Toby grinned. "I think I will. I love you. You know that, right?"

"I do. Love you too." June dragged herself upstairs and dropped her shoes in the closet. She cranked the hot water tap, closed the bathtub plug, and went to hang up her clothes. At the last minute, she grabbed the book Laura had recommended off her night stand. She might as well read more about charting her temperature to get a better fix on her cycle. Maybe if she had a pile of paper to show her, Mom would believe that June was doing everything she could think of to do.

12

The water turned on upstairs. Toby drummed his fingers on his leg. Should he go up? June had given the distinct impression on the way home that she wanted to be alone, but sometimes she gave off that vibe when what she really wanted was for him to hang out with her. If he didn't choose right they were in for another off-the-wall argument that left him scratching his head. The water shut off. Off-tune humming drifted down the stairs, along with a few random splashes. Face value. He was going to take her at face value and call his dad and watch the game. At least if they argued later he could fall back on the whole 'I did what you said to do, dear' defense. She rarely bought it, but he was going to keep trying.

Settling in his recliner, Toby clicked on the TV and flipped through the channels until a game caught his eye. He didn't have a particular team he cared about, much to the dismay of his coworkers who were either rabid Redskins or Cowboys fans. The DC area seemed to require you to care about one of those two teams. On principle, he steered clear of both. His parent's phone continued ringing, meaning they were probably on another call and ignoring the call waiting, so he sent his dad a text letting him know he was up for some football and to give him a call when he had a chance.

The phone rang almost immediately.

"Hey, Dad. That was fast."

"Um...it's Gareth."

Toby checked the phone's display and chuckled. "Sorry. Just texted my dad to call when he had a chance, I didn't even look at the ID. Missing me already? It's been what, an hour?"

"Yeah, yeah. But seriously, I probably don't have much time, I'm on an ice cream run. Betty has decided that it couldn't possibly be Thanksgiving without ice cream on her pie. Of course, I have no idea where I'm going to find someplace open. All the stores nearby were going to close at noon or one."

"Fun. Try the 7-11, I doubt they close at all today."

"Yeah, that's next on my list. Frankly I'll be fine if it takes me a while to get back. What are we going to do about her?"

"None of the options I can dream up are legal."

Gareth snorted. "We're on the same page. The insults continued after you left, just switched to July instead of June. Oh, and apparently the fact that I'm experimenting with facial hair is disrespectful."

"Seriously? A beard is disrespectful? I'd love to hear that logic."

"There was no logic. And the fact that Jules is the one who suggested it in the first place has no bearing whatsoever. How's June?"

Toby sighed. "Not sure. She went upstairs to take a bath. I think she's doing okay, but I'm still trying to figure out if I'm supposed to check on her or leave her alone. It's hard, because I don't want her to stress out. If God gives us a baby, then great. But if not? I'm okay with that, too. I don't understand why she, or her mother, are getting worked up about it. Yes, we're nearing the six month mark, but this isn't the dark ages where your usefulness was determined by production of an heir and a spare, you know? And with the mess she's got going on at work right now, I don't know how she'd handle the hormones of pregnancy on top of everything else."

"Work's not getting better? July said she thought it had at least leveled out."

"Nope. Keeps getting worse. It's tough, because she loves the work she's doing, but she's started to dread getting up in the morning. It's hard to watch and I don't know how to help. I tried to suggest she start looking for something else...that didn't go over as well as I'd hoped."

"That makes me even more sorry about this afternoon." Gareth paused and cleared his throat. "Which brings me to my main question—are you guys really okay with us? Jules keeps saying that June seems distant and on and on...and I really don't want to get involved, but it's bugging her."

Toby glanced at his cell phone as a text came in from his dad. He quickly texted back before speaking. "We're good. June's struggling, but she's also struggling with the fact that she's struggling. She wants to be happy for you, and I think she is, deep down. She's just disappointed that it hasn't been as easy here. Not that a miscarriage is easy. You know what I mean, right?"

"Yeah. Okay, I'll tell July."

"There's one other thing...and I'm pretty sure I'll be in the dog house if she finds out I mentioned it, but she thought she was pregnant about the same time as you all announced yours. The tests were all negative, but everything else seemed to point to it. Now the doctor's confirmed that no, she's not, and she's taking something this week that's supposed to get everything started back up. But she's freaking out that her cycles are getting longer and she doesn't want to talk to July about it. Which means I'm getting way too much information about this stuff right now."

Gareth's chuckle was laced with sympathy. "Maybe that's what July's been picking up on. Any idea why she doesn't want to talk to her sister? That's just weird. They share everything."

"Not everything." Toby swallowed. He really didn't want to get into this, but if the girls were ever going to get back on even footing, it was likely he and Gareth would have to be involved. "Look, she's still really hurt by the secrets you all kept—more than the actual pregnancy I think—and it's not like you didn't have every right to keep a secret if that's what you felt was best, but the word 'betrayed' crops up quite a lot. So I think she's decided that if July doesn't trust her with everything, then she's closing down the other side of the street as well."

Gareth sighed.

"I know. And I'm working on her, but it's gonna take a while. She's got too much piling on right now between not getting pregnant, gaining weight for no reason, and the work thing. I think the secrets tipped the scale one notch too far. And I have to tread lightly, because the minute she thinks I'm not one hundred percent on her side of all this..."

"I'm sorry. The secret was my idea. I thought it'd be nice for us to have something that was only for us, at least for a little while."

"I get that. I don't know what else to say though. And for the sake of clarity, you have to know I'm going to summarize this conversation for June."

"All right. Well, tell her I'm sorry again, would you? For all of it?"

"Will do."

Toby set the phone down and let his head fall back. This was such a mess. Why couldn't June and July hash out their problems like grownups? Because they were sisters. Being twins complicated it further. But why couldn't June take it as it came? Sure, women were wired to want children, but did it have to be at the expense of everything else? Wasn't there enough else in her life to make her feel complete without them?

WHEN JUNE CAME DOWNSTAIRS, bundled up in flannel pajamas and smelling of lavender bath salts, Toby filled her in on his conversation with Gareth. He'd learned early in their relationship that if he was going to get involved in an issue between the two sisters, it had to be with complete transparency. Trying to sneakily push one way or the other was guaranteed to backfire.

June shook her head. "Unbelievable."

"Which part?" Toby clicked mute on the TV and kicked down the footrest of the recliner. At least he and his dad had managed to squeeze in one game.

"The whole thing." She perched on the arm of his chair. "Mom. July. All of it. I talked to Jules, she should know we're fine, not send Gareth off on a hunting expedition with you."

"But you're not really fine. You've said as much to me. And just like you know when she's not being completely honest with you, she could tell something was off."

"So she should've asked me."

Toby arched a brow. "Would you have told her the truth?"

June frowned and wouldn't meet his eyes.

"That's what I figured. And probably what she figured too."

"I can't believe you told him everything. Can't I have any secrets?"

"Do you really want to?"

"Of course I do. She did."

Toby forced himself to stay quiet.

June sighed. "I don't know how to trust her anymore. I thought we were best friends, on top of being sisters. We told each other everything, there was never any question—it never occurred to me not to. And there were so many times when I was talking to her about us and how things weren't getting anywhere...she could've brought it up. She *should* have brought it up. But she didn't. Because she didn't trust me enough, I guess. I don't know."

"She didn't not trust you. I don't think it was ever about trust for her."

"Yeah, well it was for me." June stood. "Look, just let it go. I get what you were trying to do and appreciate the thought behind it. But this isn't going to get fixed in a day. Do you need a snack? I thought I might throw some cheese and crackers together."

Objections to the subject change flashed through his mind, but if he'd learned anything since they got married it was to go ahead and drop it. At least there hadn't been a huge fight. Yet. "Yeah, I could eat. Do we still have that summer sausage?"

She smiled. "We do. I'll make a plate—any movies on? I'm in the mood for something Christmas-y."

13

Monday dawned clear and cold. June stared out her office window at all the people scurrying to work, or to the mall down the street to get started on their Christmas shopping. She and Toby had taken a spur of the moment trip to the National Harbor to see the ice carvings and had made an overnight of it. Though she had vague pricks of guilt for missing church, it wasn't enough to outweigh the enjoyment of a mini-vacation. All the stress had dissipated with their laid-back time away. Until she'd gotten to work.

The first email had her blood pounding in her ears, tiny spots dancing in front of her eyes. It didn't matter that she could prove this accusation was completely made up, she shouldn't have to. Did no one in HR do any sort of due diligence before they opened an official investigation? June balled her hands into fists and shoved them into the pockets of her slacks. She'd forwarded it to Bob and was waiting on his response. But everything in her screamed that she should quit. Walk away. She was good at what she did, she'd find another job without too much trouble, and they could make it on Toby's salary. She shouldn't have to put up with this. But walking away felt like letting Anthony win. And he didn't deserve to win.

"Got a minute?"

June turned. Bob was hovering in her doorway. She gave a slight nod and moved back to her chair. "Course."

Bob levered himself into her guest chair and sighed, a deep frown etched into his features. "I think you're going to have to fight fire with fire. This latest...I don't know how else to resolve it. He's making up anything he can at this point."

"Can't you let him go?" June let her shoulders slump. She didn't want to deal with HR. At this point, how did she even find someone down there that would listen to her, let alone act on her behalf?

"Probably. But if I let him go now, with all this still unresolved, it looks bad. Really bad. If we can, we need to get him to recant. Once HR closes their file, then he's out of here. And I think he knows that. Thus his latest volley." Bob shifted in his seat. "I have to ask, even though I know the answer, you haven't touched him inappropriately, have you?"

June grimaced. "I've never touched him in any way. Not even a hand on his shoulder. I can't think of anyone at the office who I have touched, beyond shaking hands. That's just not who I am."

Bob nodded. "That's what I thought. This one, at least, should be easy to clear up. In the mean time," he slapped a sticky note down on her desk, "you need to call D'Shawna. She's the one person down in HR who I trust to be unbiased."

"Okay. I'll give her a call." She peeled up the note and attached it to her monitor.

"Do it today. Sooner than later, June. I've got a feeling this is going to get even uglier if you don't start taking steps. I'd hoped ignoring him, or trying to work around him, would make it go away." He stood and tapped her desk. "Don't put it off."

Sighing, she picked up the phone and dialed. Might as well get things started.

"So INSTEAD OF doing any actual work, I spent the day putting together documentation of my interactions with him, complaints about him I'd received from clients and other personnel, and asking my team to put together statements in my defense." June used her fork to stab at the salad in front of her and looked across the table at her sister. "How was your day?"

July chuckled. "Better than that, at least. It was nice to have a few hours completely to myself. Our house doesn't feel small when it's just me and Gareth, but when Mom and Dad are there we're constantly tripping over one another."

"I suspect that'd be the case no matter the square footage. You remember when we were teenagers? You and I would be upstairs and Mom would call us to come down so we'd be near her?"

July closed her eyes, head slowly shaking. "No, I'd forgotten that. That explains plenty. When they finally left, Gareth and I were both ready for some serious alone time. He actually took today off to recuperate."

"Is that why we're having dinner? You weren't very clear."

July looked down at her food. "Not exactly. Gareth mentioned his conversation with Toby."

June groaned.

"I want us to be okay. I don't like this."

June buried her face in her hands. This was the last thing she needed after a day like today. "I don't like it either." She looked up. "But I don't know how to fix it. I was hoping if we ignored it, we'd find our way back to normal."

"How does that work?"

June shrugged.

"Okay. So..."

"Look, I don't know, okay? I'm frustrated with the whole situation. I told you everything. I've always told you everything. And now...I don't feel like I can. Or should. Or something."

July reached across the table to squeeze June's hand. "I'm sorry. I...I should've told you."

"I want to agree. But the fact of the matter is, you have every right to keep things to yourself. We're grown, we're married... just because we've always shared everything in the past doesn't mean we have to keep doing it." June pushed her salad away.

"That's not..."

"I know. But maybe it's something we need to think about." June dropped a twenty onto the table and stood. "I'm gonna head home. I'll see you later. Say hi to Gareth, okay?"

∾

"THAT WAS A QUICK DINNER." Toby looked up and clicked off the TV. "You okay?"

"I don't know. It's been a rotten day."

Toby arched a brow.

She shook her head. She wasn't ready to talk about it. Any of it. "Can we go over the finances this weekend?"

"Course...what's up?"

June sighed. "I don't know how long I can keep up this thing at work. Bob got me started with a counter attack of sorts today but...it's not me. I'd rather walk away. And I know I can find something else, but I don't know if I can stick it out there until something else comes along."

Toby rubbed her knee. "We'll be fine. You do what you need to do. Obviously it's going to be best if you can transition to a new job, but if we have a little gap without your income, it'll be okay. It's that bad?"

"Yeah. Yeah it is. Maybe now that I'm working with someone in HR myself life will get better, but I'm not holding my breath."

"And things with July?"

June shrugged.

"Hm. That's all?"

"What do you want me to say? Both of us have valid points, it's not as if anyone is one hundred percent right or wrong. And maybe it's time for our relationship to change. We're not," she made air quotes, "'the twins' anymore. There are people who know me—and her—who have no idea that I have a twin sister. Maybe that's how it should be. At some point as you grow up, doesn't that relationship have to change?"

"I don't think it has to."

"I think maybe, in our case, it does." June slid off the arm of the sofa and dropped a kiss on Toby's forehead. "I'm going to find a snack, I didn't eat much. You want something?"

FRIDAY MORNING, June stared at the clock as the alarm beeped. She smacked the snooze and pulled the covers over her head as she rolled onto her side, curling into a ball with a groan. She repeated the process twice more before the side of the bed sank under Toby's weight.

"That's your third snooze. You're going to hit major traffic if you delay much more."

"I don't care."

Toby tugged the covers off her head. "Yes, you do. Get up, beautiful. Go forth and conquer the day."

June grunted and tugged the covers back over her head. "I'm calling in. I can't face it."

"Don't they require a doctor's note?" Toby peered into her eyes through a gap in the blanket fort.

"Not for one day. I'll tell them I'm having vision trouble."

Toby raised his eyebrows. "Are your eyes bothering you?"

"No...but I can't see myself going to work today."

Toby snorted out a laugh and stood. "Fair enough. Want me to take off? We can have a date day."

June shook her head. "Nah, you've got a client meeting. I'm okay. I just can't deal with HR and Anthony today on top of everything else."

He leaned down and gave her a lingering kiss. "All right. But tonight let's go out and do something fun. Just us."

She forced her lips into a smile. "Sounds great. I'll see you after work."

"You're sure you don't want me to stay home?"

"I'm sure. Go. I love you."

"Love you too." Toby blew a kiss from the bedroom doorway.

June followed his progress through the house as his footsteps pounded down the stairs and across the kitchen floor, pausing about mid-way, where the coffee machine was, before the door slammed and a car engine roared to life. She rolled to her other side, tugged the blankets back up around her neck, and burrowed in, her eyes drifting shut.

14

The mall was busier than she'd expected for the morning of a work day. June ambled down the corridor, trying to stay out of the way of the hurrying women pushing strollers and dragging older kids by the hand. Who knew there were so many mothers at home during the day? Or that they all congregated at the mall? Everywhere she looked there were babies, children, or pregnant women. Or pregnant women managing babies, toddlers, and children all at the same time. It wasn't fair.

She turned and peered in the window of a high-end kitchen store. Brightly colored enameled cast-iron cookware gleamed in the window, practically promising that you'd become a gourmet chef simply by owning it. It was something her mother would buy and then never use. She'd get it out and display it conspicuously when certain guests were coming over. June craned her neck to peer over the display and scan the store. At least it didn't appear to be overwhelmed by the stroller brigade. She'd go in and look around. Maybe find Christmas presents for July and Mom.

Sizzling garlic assaulted her senses as she passed through

the doorway. They were cooking somewhere in here. Maybe they had samples. If it tasted half as good as it smelled, she was in for a treat. Maybe there was something to those cheerful pots and pans after all? June wound through the shelves, noting a French rolling pin and cookie cutters in the shapes of TV-show starships. Hadn't July said something about needing a fancy rolling pin? She dug out her phone and texted Gareth. He'd know.

She spotted a kitchen at the back corner of the store with a chef—dressed in a white jacket and poufy hat and everything—manning a small electric skillet. Her mouth watered. Her phone buzzed. Gareth had sent a photo of the rolling pin, bless him. It looked exactly like what she'd seen. She let him know she was buying it and turned back to the food, bumping into a slender blonde.

"Excuse me. I'm sorry." Heat crept across June's cheeks.

"Not a problem." The woman turned and cocked her head to the side, eyes narrowing. "I know you. June, right?"

June nodded, eyebrows knit. She did look somewhat familiar. "Sorry. I'm not..."

The woman laughed. "Not a problem. I'm Lydia McGregor, from church?"

The pieces clicked into place. "Of course you are. What are you doing here?"

"The pregnancy center where I'm working is closed on Fridays, so I figured I'd take advantage of the break and get my Christmas shopping out of the way before it gets too crazy. Or if you meant here-here," Lydia gestured to the kitchen store, "I had a friend who used to work here and she clued me in about the sample Fridays. I figured hey, free snack. What about you?"

"Work's been rough. Really rough. So I'm taking a mental health day and thought it'd be good to get out of the house. Until I realized that the mall was apparently the domain of mothers in all stages of gestation during the day. I snuck in here to escape for a bit. It didn't look all that kid friendly. The snack is a bonus."

Lydia offered a tight smile. "You never realize how many pregnant women there are until you want to be one, do you?"

Tightness in June's chest loosened. That was it, exactly. "You too?"

Lydia lifted a shoulder. "Sort of. Kevin's not really on board yet, so we're not not trying, you know?"

June scoffed. "Oh yes, I know that well. I've moved past not not trying. Toby's still in that phase. He tells me not to worry about it. I'll admit I've started wondering what, exactly, would prompt him to worry about something."

"Ha. Yeah, I got the don't-sweat-it speech from Kevin on Sunday afternoon. You weren't in class, were you?"

"No." June glanced at the line for samples that was forming. "Let's get in line, then maybe...you want to grab a coffee?"

The line was noisy, forestalling conversation. June and Lydia collected their samples—small plates of meat and Asian vegetables—and headed out of the store with a quick stop at the register to pay for the rolling pin. There was a Starbucks two stores down with tables lining the exterior windows. June set her food down on an empty table.

"How's this?"

Lydia tugged out a chair and sat. "Ahh. Perfect."

June grinned. "I'll get the coffee, what would you like?"

"No I can..."

"Please let me."

"You sure?" At June's nod, Lydia rattled off a complicated coffee order.

Chuckling, June headed up to the counter. She hadn't expected to like Lydia. There had been so much gossip about the woman over the past several years, but June had never really spoken to her. Who knew Lydia was so down to earth?

"Here we are. One plain iced coffee for me, and one whatever it was you said for you."

Lydia laughed and took a sip. "Tastes right. Gold star for you. So, you missed Sunday?"

"Yeah. My mom and dad came to town for Thanksgiving and by the time all was said and done...I needed a break. Why? What'd we miss?"

Lydia stabbed some of the beef and pushed it around on the plate. "There's a baby boom in our class, apparently."

The blood drained from June's head and settled, leaden, in the pit of her stomach. She took a long sip of her coffee to restore some moisture to her mouth. She tried to force cheer into her voice. "Oh? Who else?"

"Laura, even though her youngest daughter, Grace, isn't that old. And Allison, even though they've only been married three months. Plus Ginger. But you were there for Ginger's announcement, right?"

June nodded. Three of them. All getting round, sharing ultrasound photos, talking about kicking and nausea and who knows what. How was she going to deal with that? She cleared her throat. "Well. Yay. I guess."

"Yeah...that's about how I felt." Lydia's shoulders slumped. "Thus the 'let's not worry about it' speech from Kevin."

"I suspect my sister'll be joining their ranks before too long. She miscarried last month, but they're not waiting to try again. And I shouldn't be as upset as I am."

"Don't worry about it. One thing rehab taught me is that you feel how you feel. What you do with those feelings, well that's the important thing. But it's okay to go ahead and feel them."

June's eyebrows lifted.

"I'm sure you know all my sordid history. I don't even try to hide it; the gossip circuit was pretty thorough." Lydia shrugged.

"Besides, it's part of my life and it's why I'm where I am now so...no point getting too worked up about it."

"Fair enough. Maybe being around all those pregnant women every Sunday will help somehow."

Lydia snickered. "There's a thought. Though if that theory holds, the fact that I work with pregnant women—and let me tell you, that's just a joy sometimes when they're there because they have what you want and they don't want it—should have given me ten or eleven children by now."

"Why is that? You're the pastor's daughter...why does God give children to people who don't deserve them? Or at least don't want them...I guess I can't say who deserves them or not."

"I don't know. You should ask my dad. I'm sure he'd have some thoughts."

"Why haven't you asked him?"

Lydia sighed and tipped her coffee cup up to get the last drops. "I haven't really told anyone we're trying...I guess I figure it opens the door to a conversation I'm not ready to have."

LOADED DOWN WITH SHOPPING BAGS, June pushed open the door and stood still. Nothing but silence. Good, she'd beaten Toby home, which gave her time to hide his Christmas gifts. Though he'd probably stumble across them no matter where she put them. He had an annoying knack for that. Still, this year she had the perfect hiding spot as long as she could stash the loot when he was out of the house.

"Toby?" No answer. June grinned and set the bags down by the kitchen island then squatted next to them and opened the cupboard. She pulled out the enormous stock pot her grandmother had given them as a wedding gift. She'd never yet needed something that held, what, ten gallons? If she ever wanted to boil a twelve pound turkey, she was set. Beyond that?

No clue. But it did hold quite a few Christmas gifts. She tucked them in and put the lid back on then wiggled it back into its spot. Perfect. She took the rest of the gifts upstairs and hid them in her closet.

Toby should be home soon. He'd mentioned wanting to do something. Which meant she probably shouldn't change into something more comfortable. Sighing, she slid out of her shoes and stretched out on the bed. She hadn't expected to have such a nice time with Lydia. After they finished their coffee, they'd wandered through some shops together. It was nice to have someone understand. Someone with no vested interest either way, so June could be completely honest about how she felt. Even though those feelings weren't always pretty.

What was she going to do about the small group though? There was no way she could keep going to that class when half of the couples were expecting. Could she? Would Toby even consider looking for some place else? He was happy with this class. And teaching wise, so was she. But all those babies...

"Hey." Toby sat on the edge of the bed, grinning. "Been in bed all day?"

"I did all my Christmas shopping, thank you very much."

"Ooh." Toby looked around the room, lips pursed. "Time to start hunting."

June slapped his arm. "Don't you dare. It's like you enjoy spoiling surprises."

"Doesn't spoil it at all for me. Plus I get the anticipation of knowing that I'm getting something great."

"Well, you're getting something great. So just anticipate it without ruining it, okay?"

"No promises."

June frowned.

"What? I can't promise. Most of the time I don't have to look all that hard. You have to admit your hiding skills are not very well developed."

"Not this year. This year I found the perfect spot."

"Hm. A challenge."

"No. Not a challenge." June giggled, grabbing at his arm as he stood. "Toby! Leave it alone."

Laughing, he sat back down. "For now. In the mean time... ready for dinner? I made reservations."

"Reservations? Fancy." June glanced down at the jeans and sweater she wore to the mall. "Do I need to change?"

"Nope. You look amazing. As always."

"Flaterer." She grinned. "I'll get my shoes. Where did you say we were going?"

"Didn't. It's a surprise."

"How come you get to have surprises but I have to fight to keep mine?" June found her shoes and checked her hair.

Toby shrugged.

Before long, they were back near the mall.

"Where do you need reservations around here?"

Toby grinned and pulled alongside what looked like an office building, though there was a valet stand, complete with red-jacketed workers, at the curb. "We've been talking about coming here for years."

"Wait. Is this the Brazilian steakhouse?"

He nodded and opened his car door as the valet rounded the hood. He accepted a ticket and circled the car, opening June's door and offering her his elbow. "My lady?"

She laughed. "You're a goof. A wonderful, thoughtful goof."

When they were seated and the waiter had explained how to signal when you were ready for the meat bearers to visit your table, June glanced around at the dim and quiet restaurant. "This is really nice. I don't know how they manage to combine linen table cloths and a casual atmosphere, but they've hit on it."

Toby nodded and tapped the meat signal. "Did you want to visit the sides buffet, or just get started with the meat?"

June inhaled as a waiter passed behind her with sizzling chunks of steak wrapped in bacon. Her mouth watered. "Flip that puppy over. Why use up room on salad?"

"There's my girl." Toby flipped the signal so the green side was up. "How was your day off?"

Between bites of the variety of skewered meats that came by, June told him about running into Lydia at the mall and their conversation and shopping excursion afterward. She set her fork down and held his gaze. "I don't know how I'm going to handle it, Toby. Especially not once July's pregnant again. It's like something sharp gets lodged right here," she pressed her breastbone, "when I think about it."

Toby sighed. "How do you know you're not going to be joining them, too? I think you're borrowing trouble and worrying for no good reason. When the time's right, it'll happen."

How did you argue with that? Obviously there was an element of truth to it, but it didn't make her feel any better. Plus there was her chart. Something was definitely weird with her temperatures compared to all the examples in the book. Hers was a flat line, a few little jiggles here and there so far, but nothing like the clear thermal shifts that were supposed to be there. She didn't have a pattern yet. She hadn't been charting long enough. But her gut told her something was very, very wrong. Should she even try to explain that to Toby?

"What if it doesn't?" June stabbed the steak on her plate but left it dangling off her fork. The heaviness in her chest and stomach had sent her appetite packing.

Toby set down his fork and gave his plate a little push. "Then we'll figure something out. But we can play 'what if' forever and never get closer to anything worth worrying about. I'm getting tired of this conversation. There's more to life than babies, and you used to enjoy talking about that stuff. Now it seems like everything circles back around to you not being pregnant. What if we can't have kids? Are you going to mope for the rest of your life? Because I'm not sure I'm okay with that."

"What does that mean?" June hissed. The couples nearby were glancing their way after Toby's tirade.

"Nothing. It doesn't mean anything except that I miss having a wife who had more to think about than the fact that she wasn't pregnant. And I miss feeling like I mattered to you as more than a potential sperm donor."

June's jaw dropped. "What...how...when...?" She balled up her napkin and dropped it on her plate. "You've lost your mind if you think that's how I feel."

"Couldn't prove it by me. Think about it. Really think about the conversations we've had in the last few weeks. If you weren't complaining about work, you were griping about not being pregnant or about the fact that someone else was. That's it. You don't even ask about my day anymore."

"I do too." Didn't she? She searched her memory but came up blank. Still, it wasn't as if that meant anything. She asked him about his day all the time, as well as all kinds of other things. "And even if I don't, it doesn't give you the right to dismiss and belittle my concerns. Would it kill you to try to understand how much this hurts me?"

"Fine, you're hurting. I get that. But I'm not sure exactly what you expect me to do about it." Toby's voice rose above the quiet murmur of the restaurant.

June caught a flash of a white shirt and black vest darting from behind the host stand and, in seconds, the maitre d' was at their table.

"Is everything all right, Sir, Madam?"

"Yes. Of course." June forced a tight smile. "But I think we're ready for the check." She flicked her gaze to Toby. "I'll be outside."

"June." Toby half stood, a resigned sigh obvious in his voice. "Just sit. Stay."

What was she, a dog? She shook her head and held out her hand. "Give me the valet ticket. I'll have them get our car."

She snatched the ticket from his fingertips and strode from the room ignoring his objection. Sperm donor? Maybe he'd feel less like that if he actually cared about the outcome of the whole process instead of dismissing it and her feelings. Or if he bothered to have feelings of his own. They'd agreed that this was what they wanted before they even started trying. Now he was going to try and make it sound like she was on some kind of crusade and dragging him along against his will? Nuh-uh.

The valet brought the car around as Toby pushed through the doors, hands stuffed in his pockets. Without a word, June climbed into the passenger side and slammed the door. She turned to look out the window, arms crossed.

"June..."

She didn't turn. Didn't acknowledge him. The words she wanted to say...it was better to keep them to herself, no matter how much she ached to let them fly.

"Fine. Great." Toby jammed his foot down on the accelerator, pushing her back in her seat.

15

Toby glanced at June out of the corner of his eye. She was acting as if everything was fine, but they hadn't discussed their argument all day yesterday or today. He hadn't heard much of the sermon this morning, his thoughts too noisy for anything external to work their way through. Now he was missing the majority of their Sunday school lesson as well. Why'd he even bother coming to church? He looked at her again. How was she able to smile and act so pleasant with all this tension humming between them? He could barely think straight.

"You all right?" Gareth jabbed Toby with his elbow as the class finished.

June stood and crossed the room without a backward glance. Toby watched as she sat next to Lydia and the two women began to laugh.

"Not really." Toby sighed and tore his gaze away from June. "We had a big fight—at least I think it was a big fight—Friday night, and she hasn't brought it up since."

Gareth's eyebrows shot up. "That's unusual. She and July are usually the queens of over-analysis and discussion."

"Exactly. I was geared up for another confrontation all day yesterday and it never happened. I even tried to bring it up, subtly, and nothing. She keeps changing the subject."

"Maybe I don't understand the situation, but why is this a bad thing? She let it go. You can too. Right?"

Toby pursed his lips. Maybe that was true. Maybe he was the only one holding on to the fight. He looked across the room at June. She was watching him. He offered a tentative smile. The look she gave him said enough. "She hasn't let it go."

"Don't know what to tell you then. But I have to think, given the alternative, maybe this is better?"

"No. It's not. It's like there's a cloud in the air and you can't get out from under it."

Gareth clapped Toby on the shoulder. "Then you have to force the issue. You can't let it fester. That's not good for either of you."

Toby sighed. "I know. I was hoping she'd be the one to do it."

Gareth snickered. "Chicken."

"Yeah, maybe. But it was bad...I said things..." Toby sighed. "Clearing it up's gonna be awful."

"Gonna be even worse if you let it go on, man."

TOBY SLOWED as the light turned yellow, then red. He looked at June. She'd been chattering about inconsequential observations the entire time they'd been in the car. Did she think filling the air with sound would somehow help? "I'm sorry."

She stopped talking and cocked her head to the side. "It's fine."

"No it isn't." He sighed and accelerated gingerly, recalling his annoyed drive home from the restaurant. "I didn't mean what I said Friday night. I'm sorry I got so frustrated. Will you forgive me?"

"Of course." She flashed him a smile that didn't reach her eyes and then continued her recounting of whatever it was she and Lydia had talked about after class.

He didn't even bother trying to listen. There was definitely something not right. Gareth had been dead-on when he said the girls were all about hashing things out. Most of the time any apology was followed by an interrogation, some sort of escalation, and then, finally, forgiveness. He didn't love the process, but he'd grown used to it. And by the time it was finished, he knew without the shadow of a doubt that he was truly forgiven. Now? She was humoring him. Which meant she was still angry, or hurt...or both. His shoulders slumped. What did he do now?

"Grilled cheese okay for lunch?" June had her door open before he'd even put the car in park in their garage.

"Sure. Sounds great." Toby cut the engine and watched her go inside. He leaned his forehead on the steering wheel. How was it possible to cause that much damage to a relationship with two sentences? Even still, knowing how much he'd hurt her, he stood by the idea behind his words. He missed the carefree, happy woman he married. It wasn't fair that the baby thing was coming to a head at the same time as everything going to pot at her office. And if the truth was told, he wasn't handling either of them well. The problem, of course, was that he wanted to fix it—and neither one was something he could fix.

Stifling a groan, Toby pushed himself out of the car. Sitting here wasn't going to solve anything.

June looked up from buttering bread as he came in. "You all right?"

"I'm really not, no." He leaned against the kitchen island. "It's like we lost our footing and I don't know how to get it back."

She shook her head and went back to the sandwiches. "You're over thinking. You apologized. It's fine. We're fine." June dropped the buttered bread into a pan on the stove and added cheese and the top slices. "Why don't you go see if there's anything good on the DVR? We can do some TV catch-up while we eat."

Toby gave her a long look. Was she really trotting out the 'it's fine we're fine' speech? It wouldn't feel like she was a million miles away if it was true...would it? But what was he supposed to do about it? Start a fight to prove a point? Yeah, that wasn't happening. Fine. They'd play it her way. He headed into the den. Maybe somehow sandwiches and mindless television would make it better.

16

June booted up her laptop, her stomach twisting into knots. Any relaxation she'd managed on her mental health day had evaporated at dinner on Friday. The underlying tension in the house for the rest of the weekend hadn't helped. Toby had tried to make amends, sort of. But there wasn't a way to undo what he'd said. So really, what was the point? She knew where he stood now...she needed to figure out what that meant in terms of their relationship. She wanted a family, yearned for it, but not with someone who wasn't as invested in it as she was. Had she made a mistake marrying him? No. No, she loved him. She still believed God had brought them together. So what did it mean that they were on two entirely different pages when it came to children?

She typed in her password and opened up her email. She wasn't going to think about this right now. The mess her personal life had become wasn't something she was going to unravel quickly. Time to see how she was faring in the mess of her professional life.

At least her email filters were still working. That was the only positive she could come up with as she stared at the two hundred unread messages. Half of them were things she could delete or file for future reference—updates on the open enrollment period for insurance and stuff like that. The other half... she sighed. What was wrong with that man? Wasn't her being out of the office his dream? If he was successful in his crusade to get her fired—because it was clear that was his end goal, even if it wasn't clear to anyone else yet—then she'd be out of the office permanently. Would he still see it as a personal affront that she wasn't there to answer his questions?

June added Bob and D'Shawna, the woman she was working with in HR, to the blind carbon copy line and addressed Anthony's questions. Several times she paused, reread what she'd typed, and edited it to ensure her frustration wasn't seeping through. Or at least less of it. Some of the questions...well, she included the original email as well. Surely Bob would realize that someone asking these questions had no clue what he was doing? If she had to choose a single word to describe Anthony it would be "unqualified." How had he gotten hired in the first place?

She checked the time and rolled her head to ease the cramps in her neck. Two hours. It simply shouldn't take two hours to deal with email after a single day off. There had been a few legitimate questions from other members of her team that she'd answered as well, but the bulk of them were a waste of her time. Why hadn't Anthony gone down the hall to ask another team member on Friday? She chewed her lip. If he'd spent all day sending her email, had he gotten anything productive done? They had a deliverable due before Christmas and it needed to be ready for internal quality assurance in another week if they were going to be on time.

Swallowing the acid that crept up her throat, she opened a secure connection to the lab fileserver. Her head began to pound as she scrolled through the files. Clenching her fists, she pushed away from the desk and stood at her window, willing herself to take deep breaths. June banged her head against the glass then let it rest there, the cold seeping into her. Not only had he not accomplished what he needed to get done, he'd undone at least four things that had been working. Things that he'd originally programmed that never worked that June had assigned to other team members to fix. Their fixes were now gone, replaced with his original buggy work. Who did that? Who willfully sabotaged their team? She forced back the scream building in her chest and went back to her desk to find an open conference room and schedule a team meeting.

JUNE SHUFFLED into the den and flopped on the couch next to Toby.

"Long day?" He hit mute on the TV and shifted to face her.

She nodded. "Long and terrible. I know they say people still have bad days in Australia, but I'm seriously considering moving there anyway."

Toby slung his arm around her and pulled her closer. "Do I get to come?"

She dropped her head on his shoulder. "I guess. If you're good."

He smiled and kissed the top of her head. "I made you dinner, does that count?"

"Yeah. But I'm not hungry. I'll take it for lunch tomorrow."

"You've got to eat something."

"Eh. I'm fine." She curled her feet up under her. "What are we watching?"

Toby frowned. "At least tell me about your day."

June sighed. "It started with the discovery that Anthony undid three week's worth of work. Then a team meeting, to which I also invited Bob and D'Shawna simply to cover my tail. And it's good I did, because Anthony showed up with his HR lackey in tow as well. The two HR people dominated the meeting and, consequently, the code still isn't fixed and at this point it's unclear if we're going to be able to fix it because Paula feels Anthony needs to be given the opportunity to fix it himself. Even though he was already given that opportunity and he insists there's nothing wrong with his code because it compiles. And sure, it compiles, but it doesn't do what it's supposed to do."

She cleared her throat and took a deep breath to ease the tightness in her chest and pounding in her temples. "Which is what I said at the meeting, without yelling, mind you, despite how very desperately I wanted to yell because the whole situation is infuriating. Then he says how he wasn't given clear specifications of what the code should do, at which point the rest of the team jumped in to say he was insane and documents were pulled out and things went back and forth. Now he seems to at least understand what he was supposed to have done, but he said he understood the first time I assigned that segment to him. So...we'll see. He gets a week to try again while the rest of us spin our wheels because we need that working before we add to it."

"How is it possible that the two HR people didn't see how incompetent he was from that?"

June shrugged. "D'Shawna seems to get it. Paula seems stuck on the fact that he's Asian. Somehow that's supposed to matter. Even though I'm pretty sure it's *not* supposed to matter. Besides the fact that there's another Asian as well as an African-American on the team, neither of whom have a problem with me because they actually know what they're doing."

"Ugh. That sounds terrible. I'm sorry." Toby ran his hand up and down her arm.

"Thanks." Hopefully they could let it drop now. She was tired of thinking about her day and wanted to relax and unwind. Their argument from Friday niggled the back of her mind. "What about you? How was your day?"

"Nothing to write home about, just a typical day." He unmuted the TV as the show came back on.

That was it? Should she probe or could she leave it alone? She didn't really want to hear any more details about his perfect job with his perfect coworkers who all loved him and got along. That was snotty...but still true. She was leaving it alone. And the next time he said something about her not asking about his day, she was going to remind him of this. 'Cause if he wanted to talk about it, he had to respond when she asked.

JUNE STOOD in the doorway and watched as women ranging from their mid-twenties to eighties swarmed the buffet table that lined the far wall of the room. What was she thinking?

"Hey, you made it." Lydia hurried across the room, empty paper plate in hand. "I figured you'd find a reason to bail on me."

June laughed. "I was just trying to come up with one. There are so many people here."

"That's generally the idea behind a women's ministry fellowship—get all the women in the church together to fellowship. Is your sister coming?"

"She said she'd try. Being the more outgoing of the two of us, she'll probably enjoy herself if she does come." June let her gaze roam over the crowd again and her stomach constricted. "How long do I have to stay?"

Lydia chuckled. "It's not that bad. Come on, there's good food over there." She grabbed June's arm and dragged her toward the buffet line.

"I'm really not hun..." June trailed off at Lydia's look. "All right, all right."

They filled their plates and found empty seats at a table near the back. The women already seated smiled as June and Lydia sat, then continued their conversation. When there was a lull, one of the ladies, who looked to be in her mid-thirties, spoke.

"Hi. I'm Gail. Are you two new to the church?"

Lydia's eyebrows shot into her hair line, but she shook her head. "No, I've been coming here basically all my life. I'm Lydia. Nice to meet you."

June cleared her throat to cover the laugh that wanted to escape. "June. Hi. Toby and I have been coming off and on for five years, since we got married."

Gail introduced the other women who all smiled politely before continuing to talk amongst themselves. "So are you in a small group? My husband and I lead a group for married couples if you don't have a place."

"I'm already in the small group her husband is leading." June gestured to Lydia.

"Oh, how lovely." Gail smiled. "Do either of you have children?"

There it was. What was that, four sentences? June's smile froze. "Not yet, no. You?"

Gail spent the next ten minutes telling them about her three children. No wonder the other women at the table were having their own conversations. They were probably all too familiar with Gail's Stepford children. Apparently they were best friends with one another and loved broccoli. June focused on her plate, shoveling in food as soon as her mouth was empty to avoid voicing the sarcastic comments that leapt to mind.

"So what's keeping you from starting a family?"

June choked on the bite of sausage ball she had in her mouth, and she sprayed little dry bits of biscuit onto the table.

Lydia pounded her between the shoulder blades. "Let me go get you some water."

June glared at Lydia's retreating form. Chicken. She cleared her throat, eyes still watering from the unexpected inhalation of food. "Just waiting for the time to be right." True enough, as far as it went. Toby would approve of the answer at least.

"Oh, honey." Gail shook her head and scooted in. "It's never going to be the right time to have kids. You're never going to magically be ready. You have to jump in with both feet and trust God to provide."

"Mmm." June bit the inside of her lip and forced the corners of her mouth upward. A flash of movement at the door caught her eye. Thank goodness. "Would you excuse me, Gail? My sister just got here. It was really nice to meet you." She stood and grabbed her plate. It didn't matter if it was obvious she was fleeing. She didn't care, she had to get away from Gail. She dropped her plate in a trash can on her way to the door and brushed her hands on her pants. "Boy am I glad to see you."

July arched a brow. "That bad? Already? Did I miss the speaker?"

"No. They haven't even started the program. I just made the mistake of sitting down with someone who, apparently, has all the answers when it comes to family building."

July's mouth formed an O. "Bet that was fun."

"You have no idea." June rolled her eyes. "And Lydia had been sitting with me but ran off as soon as the interrogation started."

"Traitor."

June chuckled. "Exactly. You hungry? The food's pretty good."

"I ate at home. Gareth made French toast."

"Ooh. I would've stayed for that, too. We should look for seats then. But not over there." June jerked her head toward the table where she'd been sitting. Gail was now deep in conversation with the other women and the seats she and Lydia had occupied were filled. She glanced around the room for another open table and her gaze landed on Lydia chatting with her mother. "Have you ever officially met Lydia?"

July shook her head.

"Come say hi then, and maybe we can find three seats together." June hooked her arm through July's as they crossed the room. Lydia and Mary quieted as they approached and June smiled. "Thanks for the water, Lydia."

Lydia hunched her shoulders. "Sorry."

"Lucky for you, my sister showed up so I could make my escape." June pulled July into the circle. "July, this is Lydia. Lydia, my twin sister, July."

"Great to meet you officially. I've seen you in small group and always wanted to come say hi, but you know how crazy it gets when class lets out."

"Me too. Not a problem." July smiled.

"This is my mom, Mary Brown. Mom, June and July. You remember I mentioned June the other day?"

"Of course. It's lovely to meet you both." Mary glanced at her watch. "I should go get things moving or we'll be here all day. Why don't the three of you see if you can find a table with four seats and I'll come join you after making all the introductions?"

17

While she waited for her sister to arrive, July closed her eyes. The warmth of the sun bathed her face. The courtyard was full of office workers enjoying the milder weather of early March. Everyone seemed glad to shrug off their heavy winter coats and do more than rush from car to building and back again. She certainly was. The winter had been odd...Christmas especially. Mom and Dad hadn't flown out and no one had gone home—Thanksgiving had been bad enough that no one wanted a repeat. But June and Toby hadn't come by like they usually did either. Things continued to be strained between her and June. And there didn't seem to be a solution. She'd tried everything she could come up with. Finally, Gareth had convinced her to let it go. But it hurt.

"Hey. Sorry I'm late." June plopped onto the bench with a heavy sigh. "Gosh it feels good out here. I'm ready for spring."

"Me too." July looked over her sister. She seemed brighter than usual. Happier. "What's up?"

"It's that obvious?"

July's stomach clenched and her smile froze. "A little, yeah."

June wiggled in her seat. "I think I may finally have the final piece of ammunition to get rid of Anthony."

A laugh bubbled out of July's throat as her insides relaxed. "Oh?"

"He took on a major deliverable. Fought off any offers of help, said he could handle the whole thing. I made sure Bob and HR were there when he chose it. It's documented every which way to Sunday that he had offers of help and that he could have chosen to share the responsibility but he refused. I think he thought this would prove his worth and ability—and it would've if he hadn't screwed it up. His work is due by close of business today and before I came here, he was in my office begging for extra time."

"You said no? Can't he get you in trouble for that?"

"Huh-uh. I've finally learned how to play the game. I put on a very serious and concerned face, like this," June pursed her lips thoughtfully and drew her eyebrows together, "and said, 'Let's go talk to Bob, see if he can get the customer to approve that.' So we went down the hall to Bob's office and he called the customer—with a cheery glint in his eye, mind you—and asked about an extension. And the customer went through the roof."

June's laugh was practically a cackle.

"Oh no." July's eyes widened.

"Oh yes. Bob had it on speaker phone. You should've seen Anthony's face. I wish there'd been a way to take a photo, it was priceless."

"It's probably wrong to enjoy someone else's misfortune as much as this, but after all he's put you through...that's sweet, sweet justice."

"Exactly." June grinned. "So the long and the short of it is that if he doesn't get it in by COB—their COB, mind you, not however long he tries to work today, they made that clear—they're going to invoke the penalty clause of the contract. And it's a doozy. I'm not excited about that aspect of things, but maybe getting a pinch in their bottom line will make people at our company finally realize that *I'm* not the problem."

July chewed on her lip. "Won't you get in trouble as his team lead? Shouldn't you have been managing him better to make sure that he was on target, that kind of thing?"

"That's the beauty of HR being involved for so long. They made it pretty clear that I wasn't allowed to do that, particularly with this deliverable. So I should be safe. Even if I get a slap on the wrist, that's the most it'd be. After the last three months, if I have to deal with a little slap, I'll take it. Especially if it means he's out of there."

"That's so great. I almost feel a little bad for him...but then I remember how badly he's been tormenting you and I get over it."

June chuckled. "Yeah, right there with you. What's new with you? How come you weren't at church this week?"

"Neither of us were feeling great. Plus, we're thinking of maybe looking around again."

"How come?"

July frowned. She couldn't tell June the real reason. It was too hard to be in the same small group when their relationship was so strained. Throw in all the women starting to show—what were there, four now? Why hadn't she kept her mouth shut?

June raised her eyebrows. "What? It's not me, is it?"

This was the problem with being twins. What you didn't know, you could usually guess. July sighed. "That's part of it, honestly. I want us to go back to how we used to be and I don't know how to get there. Maybe you were right and we can't, but that doesn't mean I like it. And I hate going there every week and seeing you with a best friend who isn't me."

"You're still my best friend. That hasn't changed...it's just..."

"You don't have to explain. You're not doing anything wrong. It's hard. Then you throw in all the pregnant bellies..."

"I know, right?" June shook her head. "And all the 'Woe is me, pregnancy is hard' prayer requests?"

July chuckled. "And those." She shrugged. "I thought maybe a change was in order."

"Please don't. I know it's weird—I promise you I'm trying to get over myself. That's what Toby says needs to happen at least." June offered a weak smile.

"I'll think about it." July bounced her knee. Should she mention it? It was such a tiny possibility. She cleared her throat. "About that...I've been charting since you showed me that book? And if that's anything to go by I might be pregnant. It's too early to test, but there was a pretty clear thermal shift..."

"Oh. Oh that's great. Congratulations."

July let her shoulders fall. "Should I not have said anything? I didn't want to make the same mistake...but maybe it's too soon? I haven't even mentioned the possibility to Gareth yet." She ran a hand through her hair. "I did it wrong again, didn't I?"

"No. No it's good. Though maybe you should've told your husband first." June squeezed July's arm. "I'm happy for you. Even if it hurts that it's not me. You're my sister, and my best friend despite what you may think. If I can't be the one who's pregnant, I want it to be you."

July watched her sister scurry back across the courtyard toward her office building. Could you be jealous of someone and happy for them at the same time? June seemed to think so but surely one had to take precedence? Which meant what? Was she going to have to choose between having a baby and having a sister? Her hand went to her belly. If there was a baby in there, and all signs pointed in that direction no matter how much she tried to downplay them, she wasn't giving it up for anything. Not even June. Her breath caught in her throat. Hopefully God would keep that from happening.

"Mmm...it smells divine in here." Gareth dropped his keys on the kitchen counter and wrapped his arms around July where she stood at the stove. "I thought it was my turn to cook?"

July smiled and leaned her head back on his chest, still stirring the simmering sauce. "It was, but I felt like doing something nice and got home a little early so...you don't mind, do you?"

He kissed the top of her head. "Never. Especially," he sniffed again, "if you made beef Wellington?"

"Good nose. Plus mashed potatoes, gravy, and roasted asparagus."

Gareth studied her, eyes narrowing. "You're not dying, are you?"

She laughed and poked him in the stomach with her elbow. "No. Goof ball. Go change, dinner'll be ready soon."

July ignored his unwavering stare as he backed toward the stairs. Maybe she should've made something less fancy, but it was his favorite. Plus it was something she enjoyed making. She wasn't fabulous in the kitchen, but there were a few fancy things she could pull off. This was one of them. The intricacy of the Wellington challenged her and took her focus completely. Meaning she couldn't dwell on her sister or the fact that she was pretty sure one of her clients had an employee who was embezzling from them. The numbers weren't lining up like they should. A bubble of gravy burst, sending searing droplets onto her skin. She stuck her knuckle in her mouth and adjusted the temperature. It was nearly thick enough. And she should keep her mind on her job.

Gareth came back into the kitchen, his dress pants and button down exchanged for jeans and a long sleeved t-shirt. Her pulse quickened. He was so handsome. As much as she loved looking at him in his work clothes, the casual attire suited him so much more.

"Could you set the table? I thought we could eat in the dining room."

"Sure. Want to use the china?" He paused by the cabinet where their wedding china was stored.

"Only if you're helping with dishes." It was beautiful and she didn't regret choosing it, but hand washing it was a pain in the rear.

"Least I can do." Gareth opened the cabinet and starting pulling out place settings.

Once they were seated and served, July opened her mouth to tell Gareth her news. "So. How was your day?" She was a chicken. But blurting it out didn't seem appropriate. Plus she didn't know for sure...but since she'd mentioned it to June, she had to tell Gareth. For all she knew, June would tell Toby and he'd let it slip. The last thing she wanted was for Gareth to find out he was maybe going to be a dad from someone else.

He gave a half-shrug as he cut into his Wellington. "Pretty typical day. We've got a new clinical trial starting up next month, so we're making sure all the medications are in place and getting the groups assigned and so forth. Nothing earth shattering. How about you?"

"Saw June at lunch, looks like the thing at work might finally be coming to an end." She recounted the tale, leaving Gareth chuckling.

"And I think I might be pregnant."

Gareth's laughter cut off abruptly. He cleared his throat. "I think I missed that."

"You didn't." She smiled.

"Way to bury the lead, Jules." Gareth grinned and reached across the table to grab her hand. "Why just think?"

July sighed. "You remember I started charting my temperatures every morning?"

He nodded, his eyes flicking up.

"I saw that. You can scoff all you want. There was a second thermal shift today, exactly like the book shows. So, if there's anything to the *science* behind the idea, I'm pregnant. I just won't be late for another four days, so taking a test isn't going to be particularly useful yet."

"Do it anyway."

She laughed. "You're worse than me. I'm trying not to waste money. We can wait another couple of days."

Gareth shook his head. "I don't know how you're so calm about this. It's been a few months...I was beginning to worry."

"I know." She took a deep breath. She'd been worried too. "But look, it's not a for sure thing. The triphasic shift isn't a guarantee, just a likely indicator."

"Have you had one before?"

"Not like this one."

He grinned and her stomach clenched. Had she gotten his hopes up for no reason? This is why she should've kept her mouth shut when she was talking to June. But once the cat was out of the bag...she fought a groan. How did she always manage to make a mess out of this?

Gareth's grin faded to a frown. "What's wrong?"

"I don't want you getting your hopes up too much. What if I'm wrong? Or I did something wrong? Or I have an early miscarriage? There's just so much that could change..."

"It's early. I get that. But I'm still excited. And I'll deal with the disappointment if I have to. We both will. For now?" He pushed back his chair and stood, tugging July to her feet. "Let's celebrate."

18

June spread the four charts on the bed and frowned at them. Flat lined. Her reproductive system was flat lined. A humorless laugh came out more like a sob. July's charts were probably picture perfect with a dip and rise to show ovulation and now...now July had her perfect thermal shift indicating she was probably pregnant. And what did June have? Lines that hovered around a low body temperature that had given her nothing but trouble her entire life. If only she could go back in time and show the school nurse that ninety-eight-point-six actually *was* a fever for her.

She pressed her fingers into her eyes. What now? She scooped the papers back into a stack and shoved them into the cover of her fertility book. Her annual exam was Friday. She'd take the charts along and see what the doctor had to say. The book had practically a whole chapter about how some doctors didn't consider charting useful or legitimate, but she had to try. If her interpretation was right—and it was hard to imagine it being wrong when all she had was a solid line instead of the peaks and plateaus she was supposed to see—she wasn't ovulating. That wasn't going to fix itself.

At least her weight gain had leveled off. Since the scale had stopped moving, she'd bought a few new clothes, cringing each time she looked at the size on the tag. Toby still insisted she was beautiful, but she was fat and broken. How was she possibly supposed to keep her marriage together with the cards stacked like that? Add to that the fact that the list of things she couldn't talk to him about seemed to grow daily...something needed to change. It had to.

June swallowed the lump in her throat. At least the thing with Anthony was nearing some kind of solution. After she'd gone back to the office, she'd stuck around and offered to help —he'd summarily refused. He hadn't made the delivery deadline. She hadn't expected him to, but miracles happened, and he lived under some kind of lucky star to have lasted as long as he did. On her way out she'd seen that Bob was still in his office, so she'd let him know what was coming. He'd looked positively giddy. At least something was finally going her way.

"Hey." Toby stretched out on the bed beside her. "How come you're hiding up here?"

"I wasn't hiding. Just changing and I got distracted." She smiled to soften the petulant tone of her voice.

"Happens to me all the time, 'specially if you're around." He waggled his eyebrows.

June snickered. "You're cute, but you're no Lothario. Still," she scooched down and lay along his side, her head on his arm, "this is nice."

"Nice?" Toby's voice was a playful growl. "I'll show you nice." His arm tightened around her, fingers wriggling their way to her ribs.

"Stop." June laughed, writhing away from the tickling. "Uncle. Mercy."

"Take it back."

"I take it back. This is horrible. Torturous, even." She grabbed his hand to stop the tickling.

"Hmm. Maybe I'll stick with nice." Toby rolled to his side and rested his forehead against hers. "How're you doing?"

"You know, it was a pretty good day." June caught him up on the Anthony situation, barely holding back the giggles as she described Bob's face when it was clear they'd missed the deadline. "It doesn't do us any favors with this client, but I think Bob has a plan in place to make sure they realize it's not us, corporately, who dropped the ball. And if the client comes back and says they don't want Anthony on their project? Then he's out. Right now we don't have anything else for him to switch to. So he can look within the company, but he'll be out of my hair at last."

"What a relief." He pressed his lips to her nose.

"I also saw July at lunch." Should she tell him? July hadn't said not to, but if she hadn't told Gareth yet...she should've said not to say something. "She's pregnant."

Toby's face morphed into a moue of regret. "I'm sorry, sweetheart."

June let out the breath she'd been holding. Maybe he was finally starting to understand. "Thanks. It's frustrating, 'cause I'm happy for her but upset at the same time."

He rubbed her back as a tear slipped down her cheek.

"Why don't we order a pizza and put in a movie? Disconnect for a little bit."

JUNE CLUTCHED her charts in her hand and opened the exam room door. Soft murmurs from the waiting room television drifted down the hall, mixing with the clicking of a keyboard in the front office. How had she managed to pick a day when Dr. Strong wasn't booked back-to-back? Didn't matter. The doctor had been willing to have a consult after the exam, and that was all June wanted.

She scooted down the hall to the office. Dr. Strong smiled as she looked up from the files on her desk. "Have a seat, June. Let me take a look at those."

June slid the charts across the desk and twisted her fingers in her lap as Dr. Strong flipped through them.

"Hmm. I see what you mean. There are actually a couple of things that concern me. First," Dr. Strong tapped the papers, "your basal temperature is low. Ninety-eight-point-six isn't really a suggestion. It's considered normal because when everything's functioning as it should, that's where your body will be. Or at least somewhere closer than you are. Throw in your weight gain and we should go ahead and run some blood work, take a look at your thyroid function."

"Thyroid? Why would that matter?"

"It might be nothing, but often a low body temperature is indicative of hypothyroid, meaning your thyroid is underactive. So we'll take a look. The flat lines though are, as you suspected, definitely an indicator that you're not ovulating. And it's certainly a challenge to conceive when that's not happening." Dr. Strong's smile was kind.

June gave a short laugh. "Yeah. I didn't think time and relaxation was likely to fix that."

"Well, you can't rule those out completely. Stress can impact fertility. But in this case, I'd like to schedule some additional blood work at a few different points in your next cycle to get a better picture of how things are functioning. Once I've got that data, we can discuss how to proceed."

"Should I see a specialist?" June didn't want to imagine Toby's reaction to that suggestion. She'd already looked over their insurance, it wasn't going to cover much if it came to that.

"Not just yet. I can do a few things, and if it's as simple as stimulating ovulation there's no need for the extra expense."

"Simple?" Could it really be simple?

"Possibly simple, I guess I should say. There's an oral

medication, Clomid, that's often very effective. But let's start with some blood work first. I'll send you home with some reading material that lays out the various options—but don't get too caught up in all the possibilities. It's easy to get overwhelmed."

"Okay." June took a deep breath. It was good to be making some progress. Though how much time had they wasted taking the wait-and-see approach?

"Go have a seat in the check-in area and I'll send someone to come draw your blood. When I have the results, I'll have the front office set up another consult and we'll go over what we found out."

"Sounds good. Thank you."

Dr. Strong passed June her charts. "I'll make sure you get those informational papers before you go. In the meantime, try not to worry too much."

"YOU DID WHAT?" Toby was as close to exploding as June had ever seen him.

She cringed and took an involuntary step backward. "It's only some blood work. I don't understand why you're making it such a big deal."

He sighed, disbelief written over his face. "Really? You don't understand why I'm upset that you've decided to go haring off on a quest to find a medical solution to a non-medical problem?"

Her gut twisted. "It's not a non-medical problem." She slammed her charts down on the kitchen table. "If you'd bothered to listen when I tried to talk to you about this, you'd understand that these," she jabbed the papers, "make it incredibly clear that something in me is not working like it should."

"You *think*. But you have no proof other than a book that

you read more frequently than your Bible."

June swallowed as the retort hit home. Was she relying too much on something other than God? No. No, that wasn't true. "Look, just because I could stand to improve my quiet times doesn't mean that there isn't also something medically wrong here. And yeah, I only *think* something is wrong because I don't have the blood work to back that up. Yet. You want proof? I'll have it, one way or another, in a couple of days."

"We should've talked about this before you did anything." Toby crossed his arms over his chest, a frown etched into his face.

"I *tried* to. You don't listen to me when the subject of babies comes up. You tune out, wait for a lull in the conversation, and then tell me not to worry about it. Well, I *am* worried about it and I'm sick and tired of you dismissing my concerns. So I'm doing something about it. Which, by the way, I wouldn't even be able to do if my *doctor* didn't agree there might be something amiss. Then if you ever decide to get off your high horse and actually care about us having a family—or at this point, the state of our marriage—I'll have some data to back things up."

June spun on her heel and stormed out to her car. She threw it into gear and peeled out of the driveway. Had he been like this when they were dating? Couldn't have been—she never would have dated, let alone married, someone so—she sorted through a list of choice adjectives—unreasonable. She'd go with that, though it was the tamest of the words she wanted to use.

Taking a deep breath, she slowed to a stop at the edge of their neighborhood. As the pounding roar inside her head subsided, she lowered her head to the steering wheel. A beep behind her had her flicking on her turn signal, checking the traffic and making a hasty right turn. Where was she going? Didn't matter. She needed to be somewhere other than where Toby was.

19

Toby's jaw dropped as the door slammed. Did June really just storm out of the house? He waited, arms crossed. She'd come back—this was so unlike her. The revving of an engine and squeal of tires had him crossing the kitchen. Jaw clenched, he opened the door and watched as she tore away from the house. He slammed the door, the impact rattling the pots hanging over the kitchen sink. What was she thinking? How was it possible she thought *he* was the bad guy here?

He stomped into the living room and threw himself onto the sofa, punching the remote to turn on the TV. Fine. If she wanted to be childish, that was fine. Just fine, in fact. He'd wait for her to calm down and then they could discuss this like rational adults. Which is what he'd been trying to do in the first place, before she took off like a pouting teenager.

Toby flipped through the channels without seeing the images flickering on the screen. After the sixth time through the entire rotation of channels he sighed and glanced at the time. She'd been gone almost an hour. He'd expected her to be back much more quickly than that. With a frown, he turned off the TV. He wasn't being unreasonable, was he? He was okay with starting a family—but he didn't see the need to rush into anything. And if God didn't see fit to give them children, well, that'd be all right too. Ask anyone who had kids, they'd tell you all about how their life had changed. And sure, they'd say plenty of positive things, but you could pick up on the wistful regrets if you listened. No more sleeping in, no more easy travel, certainly no more spontaneous trips. He wasn't in a rush to give that up. Why was she?

His conscience prodded him. Even if he wasn't in a rush, she was—and he'd agreed, somewhat, to go along with it. He should probably be more supportive. But how? She got mad when he suggested solutions and she got mad if he said not to worry about it. What was left? Besides, he wasn't the only one in the wrong here. Just because he'd agreed to try didn't mean she could rush off to the doctor and start down a path that was bound to eat up time and money. All without any more guarantee than waiting had.

As the minutes ticked by, Toby paced the length of the kitchen. The sun set in a brilliant fire of gold and pink then darkened to the dusky blue of twilight. When the first star twinkled on the horizon, his chest tightened. Had she been in an accident? Heat washed through him, leaving ice in its wake —was she not coming back?

Hands shaking, he grabbed the phone and dialed. June's ringtone jingled faintly across the room. He punched end and shifted papers and a towel to unearth her phone. He sighed. Now what? Where would she go? He dialed again, drumming his fingers on the counter as the other end rang.

"Hello?"

"Hey, Gareth, it's Toby."

"Hey man, what's up?"

Toby cleared his throat. He didn't want to get into all the details right now—and he should've thought about that before he picked up the phone. "Um. I was wondering if June was there?"

"June? Don't think so, but I haven't been home long. Let me find July, hang on a sec."

Toby listened as Gareth hollered. His voice was muffled, but Toby made out a few words of the conversation as he waited. After a moment, July came on the line.

"Toby? June's not here—was she planning to come over? I didn't have anything planned with her that I can remember."

"No. No, just thought she might've stopped by. Thanks."

"Is everything okay?" July's voice was filled with concern.

This was the farthest from okay he'd ever been. But it was between him and June. And if she hadn't gone running to her sister...well, neither would he. "'Course. Yeah, everything's fine. Um...if she should happen to swing by, would you tell her I called?"

"Absolutely."

"Great. Bye."

Toby hung up, ignoring the unasked questions evident in July's responses. Now what?

THE GARAGE DOOR CREAKED. Toby bolted upright, his back protesting the short nap at the kitchen table. "June?" Sleep clogged his voice and he cleared his throat. "That you?"

"Yeah. I thought you'd be upstairs in bed. I was trying not to wake you." She pushed the door closed, leaning back on it until it clicked. The sliver of light from the garage disappeared, leaving the kitchen dark, with only the faint silver glow of the moon.

"Where'd you go?" He fought to keep accusation from his voice. It wouldn't help and he was past the need to argue. He simply wanted her home safe.

"Drove around, mostly. Stopped for coffee." She dropped her purse on the counter. "I was going to call, but couldn't find my cell."

"You left it here. I plugged it in for you."

"Thanks."

Toby rubbed his hands on his thighs. "June..."

She shook her head. "Can we not talk about it tonight? I just want to go to sleep."

He stared. He'd expected she'd come back with a quick apology for storming off. Then he could apologize and they'd be back to fine. When her apology hadn't come, he figured it was only fair he start things off—he'd overreacted too—but this...what did it mean?

She gave a nod and started for the stairs. "'Night."

He watched her go, a hollowness forming in his chest. Should he chase her? Force her to have it out now? He wanted to...but what good would it do, really? She didn't want to talk about it, which meant she'd get angry faster if he tried to push. He was already mentally exhausted from the fight, from her leaving, from her being gone so long. Maybe she was right and they should take a break. Advice from his father flickered through his head, a warning not to go to bed angry. But how did you avoid that when one person didn't want to talk? And what if the issue was something unlikely to be easily fixed?

TOBY CRACKED open an eye as feet padded into the kitchen. He watched as June scooped coffee grounds into the machine and got it started. She stared out the kitchen window for several minutes before crossing the room to where he lay on the couch.

She nudged his feet to the side and sat. "Hi."

"Hi." Toby scooted to a sitting position. Apparently a good night's sleep hadn't helped either of them with the new awkwardness between them. His heart sank. Was it going to be possible to mend this at all?

"I'm sorry I ran out yesterday. I...I should've stayed so we could try and talk things through." One corner of her mouth twitched up, though her eyes radiated insecurity.

He nodded, not quite able to make himself say it was okay. It wasn't okay. "Thanks."

Her eyebrows lifted. "That's it? Thanks?"

Toby scrubbed a hand over his face. "No. No, of course not. I wish you'd stayed, but given how things were going I guess I get it."

"And?"

He licked his lips. "And I'm sorry my reaction upset you."

She shook her head and started to stand.

"Wait." He sighed. "I'm sorry, okay. Can you try and understand you're not the only one who's still angry?"

"You're still angry. Great. So we're still in all-about-Toby land."

"We were never in all-about-Toby land—whatever asinine place that is—but how am I supposed to react when you come home from the doctor, shove a folder of information about assisted reproduction in my face, and start talking about all kinds of treatment options when the last thing I remember us discussing was giving it a little longer before considering talking to someone? You say you want me involved in this process and that my voice is important—that having a child is a big deal and so both parents need to be on board—and then you do an end run around me. So yeah, I'm angry."

June sank back down onto the couch. Toby held her gaze as she looked at him. What was she thinking?

"Okay. I guess I can see that. I'm sorry. It wasn't my intention to make you feel like I was going behind your back. I had my annual exam at the doctor—the one it makes the most sense to talk to about this stuff, even—and it came up. So yeah, I talked to her about it. Maybe I could've brought it up with you better though. Dr. Strong even said not to spend too much time with the information in that folder until we'd done a good bit of blood work—beyond what she did yesterday."

"You agreed to do more?" He shook his head. Did his feelings not matter at all?

"No. When Dr. Strong has the lab results back, she'll schedule a consult. That's all I've agreed to—and even that isn't set in stone. I...I could tell her I'll get back to her at a later date."

Weight settled across his shoulders as he watched disappointment cloud her features. He wasn't being unreasonable. Why did it seem like he was the bad guy? "Don't do that. You've had the blood drawn, you might as well find out what she has to say about it. Just don't make any other plans without talking to me. Please?"

She gave a rapid nod and pushed off the couch, pausing to drop a kiss on his forehead. "I'm sorry. Really sorry."

He grabbed her hand, holding her in place when she'd turned to leave. "It's okay. This is going to be all right."

She offered a smile that barely made it to her eyes and went back to the kitchen. He watched as she filled two coffee cups. He believed what he said: it was going to be all right. It had to be.

20

July cornered June when small group ended. "Where'd you go Friday night?"

June furrowed her brow. "Huh?"

"Toby called Friday night looking for you—I got the sense things weren't okay, despite his reassurance. So where'd you go?"

June lifted a shoulder. "Drove around."

"Everything all right?"

"I don't know."

July frowned. That wasn't the response she'd expected. "What's going on?"

June hesitated then shook her head. "It's nothing. Don't worry about it."

July caught her lip between her teeth and watched her sister. The right thing to do, probably, was let it go. With the way things were between them right now, she couldn't push. Not if she didn't want to widen the rift. "Okay. I'm here, you know that, right?"

"'Course." June smiled. "Any official word yet?"

A grin split July's face, her heart soaring. "Got a positive on a test yesterday. Nice dark line. I'll set up an appointment tomorrow—hopefully they'll see me a little sooner than last time."

"That's great." June gave her sister a hard hug. "Keep me posted. I'm gonna go say hi to Lydia."

July watched her sister walk away and sighed. What was it going to take to fix things between them? Should she not have said anything about the pregnancy test? But June had asked... and would've known if she had dodged the question. Was there any way to actually win? She pushed her thoughts away from her sister and wandered over to join Gareth.

"Hey. I'm ready whenever." She slipped her hand into Gareth's.

Gareth nodded an acknowledgment and returned his attention to Toby. "So now what?"

Toby shrugged. "I'm kind of hoping it blows over at this point. Since she went ahead and had the blood work done, we'll see what the doctor has to say and...I don't know, figure out our options from there. But it's like we got on a horse that's galloping at top speed toward a cliff and neither of us has the reins."

July drew her brows together. What blood work? She sent a questioning glance at Gareth.

Toby sighed. "Go ahead and fill her in. Looks like June's ready to go. I'll catch you later."

As she watched Toby cross the room to June, Gareth filled July in on the details he'd gleaned from Toby.

"Why didn't she say something? I outright asked her and she brushed me off." July frowned, her hand moving to rest on her stomach. "I don't want to have to choose between my sister and our baby."

Gareth slid his arm around her and rubbed her back. "It won't come to that. Reading between the lines, she's hurting and taking it out on anyone who pops their head up. Toby's getting the brunt of it, but you're probably second in line. I think he's got the right idea though—it'll blow over. It always does with June. Though I disagree with his stance on blood work. It's definitely time for them to do at least basic testing. And knowing what's going on doesn't mean they have to do anything. It's just information."

"Did you tell him that?"

Gareth nodded. "Not sure he agrees, but it'll percolate. Maybe the seed will take root."

July brushed her lips across his cheek. "Thanks."

She could only imagine how difficult it must be for June. With Toby as laid back about the whole thing...June must be ready to chew nails. A fight was inevitable. Hopefully they'd work through it quickly and Toby could get on board. More than anything, July still cherished the idea of her children growing up with cousins who were close in age. They'd never had that and, as a result, their extended family seemed distant and foreign. Both Gareth and Toby had cousins with whom they were close and it was a bond that at times seemed tighter than that of a sibling. She wanted that for her kids.

JULY SLAPPED her Bible closed and let her head fall back onto the top of the couch. She'd been hoping to find something encouraging to pass along to June, but there were too many passages about children to sort through. And some of them... they weren't overly helpful. Ginger had suggested the story of Rachel, but after reading it over July didn't understand how anyone would think that was helpful to a woman having trouble getting pregnant. God opened and closed wombs in that story like they were supermarket lanes. So what was the takeaway? That maybe you weren't getting pregnant because God didn't want you to? Possible, obviously, but not encouraging. Hannah's story wasn't much better—having to barter away the child you so desperately desired? Sure, God gave her more children after Samuel, but if you looked at it through the lens of hurt that came with any sort of struggle to get pregnant...it wasn't going to fly. Particularly since July was pregnant. It would be hard to convince her sister with either of those two stories that she was trying to be helpful.

"That's the fourth time you've sighed in like two minutes." Gareth looked up from across the room where he sat reading. "What's going on?"

"Ugh. Trying to find something in here to encourage June." She tapped her Bible. "And failing miserably. Have you actually read any of the stories of infertility and pregnancy carefully? They're terrible."

"Can't say I've paid over much attention. But what about Rachel? I thought God opened her womb, isn't that encouraging?" Gareth stuck his finger in his book and flipped it closed.

"It might be if it wasn't opened then closed then opened then closed...between her and Leah it's like womb roulette in that story. And Rebecca's not really any better—or Sarah for that matter. They all make it look like if you pray then God will have pity and open your womb. But what if He doesn't? Does that mean you're not praying right? Or that He's punishing you somehow? David's first wife, Michal, certainly appears to be rendered barren as punishment." July shook her head.

Gareth winced. "Not really the message you want to pass along. Though I guess you could take away the fact that God uses infertility in His plans...but maybe that'll only be comforting when you're on the other side of things. What about something from the Psalms? Like the 'you knit me together' one?"

"Hmm. That's a possibility." July flashed a grin. "Thanks, babe."

JULY CLUTCHED THE CARD. Using her best calligraphy, she'd written verses thirteen through sixteen of Psalm 139 on it. Despite having not spent much time lately practicing her "letter art," as Gareth referred to it, it had turned out pretty well. June had always been encouraging when it came to July's experimentation with different pens and nibs. Hopefully that would make the gift that much more meaningful. The purples and greens swirled and looped together as the words danced across the card. It might be her best creation yet.

June strolled across the courtyard, clutching a brown paper sack with a potbellied stove emblazoned on the front.

"Ooh. Lunch?" July nodded at the bag from a nearby sandwich shop.

"Yeah. I got the big one—want half? It has peppers though."

Saliva pooled in July's mouth and she nodded. "I brought you this."

June took the card and slipped her finger under the flap of the ornately scrolled envelope. "Pretty. You've gotten really good, when do you have time to practice?"

"I haven't been. I'm glad you like it." July wiggled the bag out of June's fingers and unwrapped the sandwich, pulling out the slightly smaller half for herself and dropping the other half back in the bag.

June tucked the card under her leg and got out her sandwich, filling her mouth with an enormous bite.

July's eyebrows lifted. "How's work? Any movement on Anthony yet?"

"Too soon, but Bob's been on the speaker phone all morning. And given the way his voice is carrying down the hall, the conversations haven't been happy." She flashed a grin. "I have a feeling there'll be something positive before the end of the week."

"That's great." July wrapped up half of her part of the sandwich. She'd eat it later. Maybe. Her stomach roiled. Or not.

June flicked her gaze over. "Not hungry?"

"Not sitting well." July swallowed the bile that was working its way up her throat. "Morning sickness isn't only in the morning, I guess."

"Oh. Right."

July frowned as her sister shut down. She hadn't intended to mention anything pregnancy related today. Possibly ever. Her stomach twisted and the blood rushed from her head. She clutched the back of the bench. She refused to pass out or vomit. She wouldn't. Not with June here. Not in public.

"You okay?"

June's voice echoed as if coming down a long hallway.

July breathed deeply through her nose. "Yeah." She swallowed as things began to work their way back into focus. "Sorry. I should probably get back to the office. I just wanted to give you that card. You know I love you, right?"

June nodded. "Back atcha." She stood and frowned at July. "Are you going to be able to get back all right?"

"'Course. It's only a block. I'm fine. It comes and goes fast."

"All right. Call my cell if that changes and I'll come find you." June gave July a quick hug and started off across the courtyard.

"June...you forgot your card."

"Oh, right." June offered a tight smile and strode back, snagging the card off the bench. "Wouldn't want to lose that. Thanks."

July watched her hurry away. Had she left it there on purpose? Sighing, she stood. When had she lost her ability to understand her twin? More importantly, would she ever get it back?

21

June tossed the card face down on her desk. Her sister meant well. But frankly she was getting tired of well-meaning people and their so-called encouragement. It was too bad she'd gotten caught trying to leave it on the bench. The artwork was gorgeous, but the actual text...ugh.

"Knock knock." Bob stood in her doorway, a grin poking at the corners of his mouth. "Got a sec?"

"Sure. Come on in."

He shut the door behind him and settled into one of the guest chairs facing her desk. "We're making some headway. The customer is beyond ticked and already has their legal department talking to ours."

June winced. "I..."

Bob held up a hand. "I don't love it either, but when I explained to the project manager why we didn't have someone swoop in and save the day he understood. I don't think our future business, or this contract actually, is in serious jeopardy. But there are penalties for missing deliverables and they're exactly right to enforce them."

Her stomach twisted. Was this going to come back on her after all? "And I'm the project lead."

"Oh no. I mean, sure, you are the project lead, but you're not responsible. You and I both have documentation from here to Sunday on this one, and even Paula wasn't able to do more than look sour when I explained to her that the buck rested squarely on Anthony's shoulders."

"So...what now?" A flutter of lightness started in her chest. Might they actually be able to get rid of him?

"For you, keep the status quo—include him in all the team meetings and document everything as usual. But I'm taking the documentation we have and setting up my case."

"What about his counter allegations about me? Am I still under investigation?"

"For the time being. That's why you keep documenting everything. But don't be discouraged. I think things are finally turning out the way they should." He hefted himself to his feet. "Chin up."

"Okay." June's phone started to ring.

"I'll let you get that. Just thought I'd keep you in the loop." Bob yanked open the door and disappeared into the hall.

"This is June." She swiveled in her chair as she picked up the handset.

"Hi June, this is Dr. Strong's office. She'd like you to come in to discuss your blood work. Is there a day this week that's best for you?"

HEAD SWIMMING WITH INFORMATION, June came home early on Thursday afternoon. She'd planned to go back to work after her meeting with Dr. Strong, but wouldn't have been able to focus. She wanted to spend some time going through the papers Dr. Strong had given her, maybe do a little poking around online as well. And figure out how to share all the information with Toby. She'd wanted him to go with her, but when the nurse called on Monday she'd gone ahead and taken the first available appointment. Toby hadn't been able—or willing —to take the time off to come along.

She sighed, blinking back tears. It was as if nothing having to do with a baby was a priority for him anymore. If it ever had been. She tossed the folder of information on the counter and kicked off her shoes, her motivation to read up on things gone. Was there any point if Toby wasn't going to participate? It took two parents to have a family. At least in her mind it did. She had no desire to be a single parent, especially since she wasn't single. Now what? She drummed her fingers on the counter before picking up the phone.

Twenty minutes later, June settled into a booth at Panera with a bagel and cup of coffee. A few minutes later, Lydia slid into the booth across from her and grinned.

"Hey. This was a great idea. I've been meaning to call all week but everything's been crazy. Kevin has a basketball game with Matt and some other friends after work tonight, so he'll be home late. This keeps me from sitting on the couch feeling sorry for myself."

June chuckled. "I'm sure you could've talked Laura and Allison into doing something."

"Yeah, probably. But since both of them are pregnant, it seems like every time we get together that's all we talk about. I have very little to add to that conversation. It could only be worse if they transitioned into labor and delivery stories... which I'm sure is next."

"Ugh. I guess I should be grateful July hasn't started with that—though she got pretty sick during lunch on Monday."

"She can't really help that."

June frowned at the reproach in Lydia's tone. "I know...it's still hard though. I'm trying. I am. She doesn't help things by giving me stuff like this though." She dug around in her purse, finally pulling out the calligraphy card July had given her on Monday.

Lydia read it, her eyebrows lifting. "I am fearfully and wonderfully made, oh this is lovely—the artwork and the sentiment."

"Really?" June took it from Lydia and glanced over the words again. "All I see is an acknowledgement that God made me broken on purpose. What's worse, how many times does the Bible say children are a blessing? And yet, this says God knit me this way, specifically, and excluded me from His blessing. How is knowing that encouraging?"

"Wow. I don't think I've ever thought about it that way. I guess I kind of see where you're coming from but...I really don't think that's the interpretation you're supposed to take. God loves to give good gifts to His children—I don't think that goes hand in hand with setting them up so they're ineligible for a blessing." Lydia reached across the table and tore a piece off June's bagel.

"Hey." June slapped Lydia's fingers. "You might be right. But it's hard not to read it that way. Throw in all the other comments I'm getting that are meant to be encouraging...why do people feel like they need to butt into my reproductive life?"

Lydia chuckled. "Wish I could say I had an answer to that. I suspect it's human nature. The people who want the best for you are going to offer encouragement that comes across flat, and the people who aren't as motivated by good things are going to find ways to make a dig." She shrugged. "It's one reason Kevin and I haven't said anything in class. After everything I went through before we got married...I can only imagine the commentary we'd get. It'd be either reminding me that, having had an abortion, I don't deserve to have children now or that God's punishing me for my sin and that's why it's taking a while. Why Kevin also deserves to suffer, I couldn't say —maybe for being willing to forgive me?"

"At least Kevin's supportive. All Toby says is that we should wait and see. I had some blood work done as part of my annual exam and he went through the roof—like I'd committed him to invasive surgery or something. But I was the one who had the needle in her arm, he didn't have to do anything. I don't get why it was such a big deal. And then today, I got the results...and he's going to flip again." June buried her head in her hands.

"I take it they weren't great?"

"Understatement of the year. Basically, she thinks I'm going to need more than the oral medications they use for inducing ovulation. She still suggests we start with them, but she said not to get my hopes up. My hormones are all out of whack and I have something called..." June wrinkled her nose, what was it? "Poly-something ovarian syndrome. Basically there are a whole bunch of undeveloped follicles on my ovaries that mess up the whole system and keep me from ovulating. And all this lovely weight gain is likely owing to it as well. She gave me a bunch of reference material that I'd planned to read when I got home...but I called you instead."

"Not that I'm ungrateful...but what happened?"

"I started thinking."

"Dangerous." Lydia grinned and tore another piece off June's bagel. When June frowned she said, "What? *You* aren't eating it."

June swiped at the hot tear that trickled down her cheek. "Toby...he doesn't want to do any kind of treatment. He's very much in the if-God-wants-us-to-have-kids-we-will camp. But if my body's broken...does that mean God doesn't want us to have kids? And if that's the case, why do *I* want them so badly?"

"Has he said that? Really? That he won't do any treatment at all?"

"Well...not in so many words." June flicked at the ragged

edge of her bagel. "But the way he acts when it comes up makes it pretty clear."

Lydia pressed her lips together. "You need to talk to him. Give him a chance to get on board. Don't assume. That's the number one thing I've learned from my mistakes in life—you can't assume you know how people will react. You have to give them a chance. If you don't, you do things you regret for a long time to follow."

TOBY'S CAR was in the garage when June pulled in. Talking to Lydia hadn't put her mind at ease as much as she'd wanted it to, but there was plenty of food for thought. She wasn't going to bring up the doctor's appointment right away. If he asked, sure, she'd talk about it, but she wasn't ready to get into another argument...and that was likely to be the result.

Pushing her lips into a smile, June stepped into the kitchen. Where was he? She'd expected to see Toby either there or in the living room. She dropped her purse on the counter. Where were her papers from the doctor? Had she moved them? Her heart sank. Toby must have taken them. No avoiding the conversation now. She could, at least, wait for him to bring it up though.

June washed her hands and started pulling out ingredients for a quiche. Maybe once it was in the oven she'd look around and see where Toby had wandered off to. With mushrooms, bacon, and onions sizzling in a sauté pan, and a ball of dough coming up to room temperature on the counter, she cracked eggs into a bowl and whisked them together with a splash of heavy cream. Should she add spinach, too? Digging around in the freezer revealed a box of frozen chopped spinach. Why not? She put it in the microwave to defrost and set to work rolling out the pastry. The tense muscles in her shoulders and back loosened as she leaned into job. When it was the correct thickness, she carefully rolled it around the pin before picking it up and unrolling it onto the quiche dish. A smile crept onto her lips as she gingerly pressed the malleable crust into the corners and pinched together a pretty fluted edge.

The oven beeped, signaling its arrival at 350 degrees. Perfect timing. At least she could still do some things right. After draining off the excess fat, June dumped the contents of the pan into the bottom of the quiche and spread them out, pausing to snag a piece of bacon and pop it in her mouth. Crunchy saltiness exploded on her tongue. Her eyes closed. Heaven.

"I saw that."

June jolted, eyes snapping open. "Sheesh. Way to give your wife a heart attack."

Toby laughed and filched a piece of bacon out of the bottom of the quiche.

"Hey. No snitching."

"Only cooks get to do that?" He leaned in and pressed his lips to hers. "What about people who are desperately in love with the cook?"

Warmth spread through her as their eyes met. No matter the petty irritations—or not so petty ones—he could still turn her insides to mush. "Oh all right. You get a pass." She thwapped his hand with the spoon as he went to get another. "A *one time* pass. Leave some for the finished product."

With an innocent grin, Toby snuck another piece and popped it in his mouth. "So where were you? Working late?"

June poured the egg mixture into the pie shell. "No. I met Lydia for some coffee after the doctor." Head bent, she glanced up at him through her eyelashes. Was he going to mention it now? Should she ask?

"Fun. I bailed on the basketball game invite—thought you might want me home instead. I, uh," he cleared his throat, "took the liberty of poking through the information Dr. Strong sent home. I'm sorry, baby."

June let her head fall to his shoulder as he pulled her into his arms. She breathed in his scent—it was a smell she'd come to associate with being home—that mixture of after-shave, soap, and Toby. She could stay like this forever. Had he finally started to see that there was an issue?

"Thanks." June gave him a squeeze and eased back. "I should get this in the oven if we're going to eat before it's too late."

"While it cooks, why don't we talk about what this blood work means and where we want to go from here."

Her heart leapt. Maybe they were finally on the same page. She slid the quiche into the oven and set the timer. "Sounds good."

June followed Toby into the den where his laptop sat on the side table, the folder from Dr. Strong next to it. Papers were spread out on the floor. "You've been busy."

He shrugged. "Once I saw that it wasn't as simple as I'd been thinking it was going to be, seemed like research was the next step."

They were so alike sometimes. That had been her initial thought, until she got derailed by worst case scenarios with him. She gathered up a pile to clear a spot and sat. "At this point, you might understand more than I do."

"I doubt that, but I can go first if that's what you want." Toby scratched the back of his neck, his gaze wandering over the stacks of research. "All right. I started with the papers from Dr. Strong that I found on the island. That gave a little information about the condition—poly-cystic ovarian syndrome—that she says you have. From there, I hit up the Internet. So, the quick summary, to see if I understood what I was reading, is that you have cysts on your ovaries that cause increased production of some hormones and decreased production of others resulting in long or non-existent cycles, most of which are anovulatory."

"Listen to you, 'anovulatory'—for those of us without a medical degree, that means I don't ovulate, right?"

He chuckled. "Right. Beyond that, there are all kinds of symptoms that can go along with this, weight gain is the only one I've heard you mention so far though. Well, that and you're not pregnant. What's frustrating, though, is looking up PCOS—that's how everyone seems to refer to this thing you've got—shows a broad range of women with it, some who have no trouble getting pregnant and others who go through the pre-IVF medications and still don't create useable follicles. And there doesn't seem to be any way to predict where someone will fall or what medication might work."

June's shoulders slumped, hollowness spreading thorough her. "So we still don't really know anything we can act on?"

Toby frowned. "It's not quite that hopeless...but it looks like it's going to be a ton of trial and error. It doesn't even seem like doctors have a standard treatment plan. Everyone kind of veers off on their own. Did Dr. Strong say anything?"

"She wants me to try Clomid. She said she wasn't positive it would work, but it was the best place to start."

"Hm. That was mentioned somewhere." He flipped through the papers near him. "I need to organize all this, I went a little print crazy. Regardless, I don't recall it being specific to PCOS?"

June shook her head. "I don't think it is—she didn't really say anything about treating that, she's more focused on inducing ovulation. She didn't seem to think the other was a big deal beyond being a bunch of annoying symptoms." The oven timer beeped before Toby could respond. "Let's talk more after dinner—I can hop online and do some research too."

22

June forced herself to look away from the pregnancy test sitting on the bathroom counter. The past several weeks had been full of prayer and research and, finally, her first course of Clomid. Despite June's request, Dr. Strong had insisted they begin with the lowest dose and follow the usual protocol, increasing only if the first course failed. Which of course it was going to. She swallowed the lump in her throat as the timer beeped. With a deep breath and a quick prayer, June eyed the test. Bold, all-caps letters screamed out NOT PREGNANT.

Toby knocked then pushed open the door, his expression full of hope. "So?"

June shook her head. Thoughts jumbled in her brain, but when she opened her mouth, only a low moan escaped. Then the dam broke. She sank to the floor and curled in on herself as sobs took her breath.

"Hey." Toby knelt and wrapped his arms around her, rocking gently. "Shh. We knew this might happen. It's step one. It's going to be okay. Maybe the higher dose will work."

June shook her head. Why wouldn't the tears stop?

"Even if it doesn't...we have options. We can find a fertility doctor..."

She dragged her hand across her face, smearing away the tears and met his gaze. "What if God just doesn't trust us...me... with kids? What if all this upheaval at work is because there really is something wrong with me and it's meant to be some kind of warning? Maybe I really am a horrible person and I'm too self-absorbed to see it? Am I missing something?"

"No. Don't even think that." He kissed her forehead and pulled her into his lap. "God has plans for us—for a hope and a future. Maybe that means children and maybe it doesn't, but either way, this process, the stuff at work, they're not any kind of reflection of you. You're beautiful, inside and out."

She leaned her head on his shoulder, wanting to believe him. But how? The Bible all but promised children as a direct result of following God faithfully. Didn't that mean infertility was a punishment for sin? Look at July—she could get pregnant, and she was a much better Christian than June had ever managed to be—she'd even considered the mission field. That thought had never entered June's mind.

Toby rubbed her back. "It's going to be all right."

Why couldn't she have that kind of faith?

JUNE SCANNED THE COURTYARD. Where was July? Her sister was always early, which was why they could usually claim a bench on a gorgeous day like today—the kind when everyone took time to leave the office and enjoy the warmth of spring. They were going to end up sitting on the low brick wall that enclosed the fountain and garden in the center. With one final look around to be sure she hadn't missed July, June sat on the wall and stretched her legs out in front of her. Despite the sun beaming down, a chill worked its way through her pants. Maybe it'd warm up as she sat—if her rear didn't freeze.

A flash of red hair grabbed her attention. July was winding her way through the lunch crowd. She looked paler than usual.

"Sorry." July frowned at the wall before looking around. "No benches?"

"I was late, too. It's almost seventy degrees, the sky is that blue that has no name, and there's not a cloud in sight. Everyone's out enjoying it." June shifted. Why did bricks have to be so hard?

July sighed and lowered herself to the wall.

"Where's your lunch?"

"I could ask the same thing." July shrugged and wiggled in her seat. "Not hungry. Maybe I'll eat it later."

"Are you okay?"

"I don't know. I..." July drew her brows together. "Sure it's okay if I talk about this?"

Pregnancy woes. Of course. Goody. June forced her lips into a smile. "Positive."

"I've been spotting—bleeding, really. And I've got...I don't know what to call it, cramps?" July's hand hovered over the right side of her abdomen. "Some kind of pain. The doctor says it can all be normal but I'm scared, June. I'm so scared."

"You can't get in to see her? Pain and bleeding doesn't sound normal—how would that possibly be normal?"

July winced and shifted again. "I'm supposed to go in tomorrow if it doesn't start getting better."

June frowned and tugged her cell phone out of her pocket. She poked her web browser and did a quick search for bleeding in pregnancy. Some spotting could be normal, and there was such a thing as round ligament pain...but that didn't sound like what July was describing. "I think you should go to urgent care. Or the ER."

"I don't want to second guess the doctor. Besides, I have all kinds of pregnancy symptoms—nausea, lightheadedness—I didn't have those before. I'm sure it's fine...I'm just overly sensitive after the miscarriage."

June bit her lip. Should she push? "If it gets worse, will you go?"

"We'll see...it...it shouldn't get any worse. It's been like this for about a week now."

"A week? That's a long time, Jules. And it's been the same the whole time?"

July's gaze shifted away from June.

Something was going on. "Jules?"

July gave the barest shake of her head, her gaze fixed on her shoes.

"What do you mean? Talk to me."

July's tongue flicked out to wet her lips. "It started as a little spotting, here and there. Pain was the same, a flinch on the side if I bent a certain way. I wasn't worried—that did feel like a normal part of everything going on down there. Now..."

"Now what?"

"It's really more than spotting and the pain..." July swallowed and her eyes locked with June's. "It's gotten bad."

"Did you tell the doctor?"

"That's why I have an appointment tomorrow instead of next week. But she also said if I am miscarrying again there's not much they can do to try and stop it."

June rubbed her sister's arm. She didn't have any words. Was it better to be able to conceive just to face the possibility that you'd lose the baby? Maybe all those negative tests were better? No. At least July had hope. She wasn't broken and useless. She hadn't been completely abandoned by God.

"I'M TAKING July to the ER. Pray for us, please." Gareth's voice was full of barely controlled desperation.

June rubbed sleep out of her eyes and sat up, glancing over Toby's snoring form to the clock. Three a.m. "Wait. What? The ER? Why?"

"She's in serious pain—it's moved from one side to her whole abdomen and now her shoulder's hurting. Something's really wrong. She's almost passed out twice. I'll call you when we know more. We just need you to pray."

"Will do. Gareth..."

"Yeah, I know. I'll call you in a bit."

June looked at the phone. Why hadn't she pushed at lunch? She put the handset back in the cradle and swung her legs over the side of the bed. Should she wake Toby? He'd pray with her, but would that really do any good? She pulled her lip between her teeth. His prayers might do more good—at least God hadn't deserted him. And it wasn't the time to worry about that. Her sister needed her, needed prayer. And June needed Toby.

"Toby." She leaned over and wiggled his shoulder.

"Ungh. Time's it?" He rolled to his back and slung an arm over his face.

"Three. Toby, Gareth's taking July to the hospital, something's really wrong. We need to pray."

"'K." He started to roll back over.

"No...I need you to do it. I...I don't think mine will be good enough."

June caught the flash of sleepy puzzlement on Toby's face before he started to pray. His words drifted around and over her, disconnected from her mind. She couldn't focus.

"Amen." Toby's hand groped across the top of the bed 'til he found hers and gave it a squeeze. "Try to go back to sleep. We'll know more in the morning. For now, we have to trust that God's got this."

Right. Trust God. She wanted to...but what was the point?

She'd trusted God with her career and that wasn't going all that well. Even if Anthony was finally on his way out, the black mark on her reputation wasn't going away. The damage was done. She'd trusted God to give her children and look how well that'd been going. Heck, she'd trusted God with her marriage and instead of someone who took her side, supported her, and sympathized she had a husband who dismissed her fears and pain and got irritated with her for having them. Sure, he had his moments of support...but she never knew if she was going to get rebuffed or encouraged. How was she supposed to trust God with her sister? July was the only thing she had left.

23

W ork was intolerable. Gareth had called back at seven while July was in surgery. Her pregnancy was ectopic and the tube had ruptured. They weren't even going to be able to do the surgery laparoscopically. Gareth promised he'd call when she was out of recovery and in her room. June was going to leave as soon as he called. Why didn't he call?

June snatched the phone before the first ring ended. "This is June."

"June, hello, it's Paula from HR. How are you today?" The woman's voice dripped saccharine.

Her heart sank. Why hadn't she checked the Caller ID? "Oh. Great. What can I do for you?"

"I was hoping you'd be able come down this afternoon for a final follow up meeting regarding the matter with Anthony. Say two o'clock?"

"I'm sorry, that's not going to work for me today. I have..."

"I was worried you were going to be like this. No matter how things ended up working, you need to understand that I'm watching you. The next time there's an issue in your department, you're going to be the first person I look into. Now, I'll expect to see you in my office at two."

"But I..." The phone was dead. She wasn't going to be there. Surely Gareth would have called by then, and she was leaving as soon as it was okay to go visit. She needed to see her sister— to know she was all right. June dropped her head back against her chair. She didn't want to bother Bob with this. He'd done so much for her already. But she was going to have to ask. No use putting it off.

She walked down the hall, stomach in knots, and tapped on Bob's doorframe.

"Come on in, June." Bob glanced up from his monitor and waved her to a chair. "What's up?"

June perched on the edge of the seat and twisted her fingers in her lap. "I just got off the phone with Paula in HR? She wants me to be at some kind of meeting at two this afternoon?"

Bob rolled his eyes. "I can't imagine what she wants to talk about. I'm supposed to be there as well. Anthony has his marching papers, his last day is next Friday, the deed is done, what else can she possibly need to discuss? Still, we should be out of there reasonably quickly."

"That's the thing. Um. My sister." She paused and cleared her throat, as her eyes filled. "My twin? She's in the hospital having emergency surgery. I wanted to go see her as soon as I got the go-ahead from her husband. It should be any minute."

Bob tapped his lips with a pen. "Mmm. If it was anyone other than Paula, I'd say I understood a hundred percent. In fact, *I* do understand. But she's going to make your life a living misery if you're not there. You're already on her list—don't make it worse, June."

June gave a short nod and stood. "But..."

He shook his head. "It's not worth your career to wait an extra hour or two, is it?"

Deflated, June turned and went back to her office. Her

message light was blinking. Had she missed Gareth's call? She rushed to her desk and punched voice mail.

"Hi June, it's Gareth. She's out of surgery and in recovery. They should have us to a room in another hour or so, depending on how she does coming out of anesthesia. They had to..." His voice broke. He paused and cleared his throat before continuing. "They had to remove the tube, it couldn't be salvaged. She hasn't quite grasped that yet, I don't think. Come when you can—they can give you her room number at the front desk when you get here."

June sank into her seat and stared at the door. She should leave. Paula could get over herself. But she wouldn't. If June had learned anything over the past months it was that Paula wasn't going to get over anything. She was going to push and concoct and drag until she found something. And since June had made her list thanks to Anthony's fantasy injuries, she'd better suck it up and stay for the meeting. At least once the man was out the door all this would be over.

JUNE PUSHED OPEN the door to the women's wing and stopped. Muffled sobbing leeched out from behind one of the doors while multiple doctors were paged over the PA. At least the antiseptic smell faded some once the doors swished closed behind her. She stepped around an empty gurney someone had ditched in the middle of the hall and mouthed the room numbers as she made her way past the nurse's station.

The door to July's room was half-open, a man's hand curved around the jamb. June pursed her lips, should she wait? Probably better to have only one visitor at a time. She leaned against the wall opposite the door. From the snippets of conversation that drifted into the hall, he was taking his leave.

"June?" Paul Brown smiled as he turned in the doorway. "She's been hoping you'd be able to make it."

"Pastor Brown. I'm so glad you could come. I know Gareth's here, but we both so appreciate you as a pastor."

He chuckled and laid a hand on her shoulder. "Thanks. Let me know if there's anything I can do, will you?"

"Of course." She frowned and watched him turn down the hall toward the exit. "Pastor Brown?"

He stopped and turned. "Yes?"

She hurried to close the gap between them. "I just...I'm wondering if you can you tell me why this happened?"

Paul cocked his head to the side. "Why?"

"Why would God do this? July...she's always lived for Him —hasn't she earned a blessing? Why does the Bible taunt us with the idea that children are a blessing and then turn around and have God withhold them, while he gives them to people who don't want them or who throw them away?" She stopped and took a deep breath. She wasn't going to yell.

Paul pressed his lips together, his head shaking. "I don't know. I do know sometimes you simply have to have faith. The rain falls on the just and the unjust, and somehow, God's going to use this for His glory."

That wasn't the answer she wanted. She wanted an explanation, some kind of justification to have it all make sense. With the barest nod in response she turned and went to July's room.

"Knock knock." She forced a bright smile.

July lay in the hospital bed, the head raised slightly. She was pale, even her hair had lost some of its fire. Tubes ran from IV bags to her arm carrying various medications and...was that blood?

"Hey. You made it."

"Couldn't keep me away. Though work tried. I'm sorry I wasn't here right when you got out of surgery. I should've called in sick, but I thought—hoped—that being productive would keep me from worrying. Then I got stuck in this meeting at two...where's Gareth?"

"He was exhausted. I sent him home. He was going to try and sleep over there." She wiggled a finger toward a long bench built into the area under the window and lined with cushions.

"Would he even fit?"

July shook her head. "That's why I sent him home. The nurse said they'd get a recliner brought in for him so he could stay tonight. He'll be back after dinner. Sit. You're making me nervous."

June perched at the foot of the bed, careful to avoid July's toes. "How are you feeling?"

"About like you'd expect, I guess. I'm still a little nauseous from the pain medication, but they gave me something to help with that...maybe it's working. At least I don't hurt. After the last week it's really nice to not be in pain anymore."

"Oh, sweetie...why didn't you do something about it earlier?"

"I was so scared I was miscarrying. I figured if I ignored it..."

June frowned and rubbed her sister's leg under the scratchy hospital blanket.

"I know, okay. I know it was stupid. And now..." Tears brimmed in her eyes, spilling over onto her cheeks. "Now I'm down a fallopian tube, so my chance of conceiving just got cut in half. If I'd acted sooner they probably could have at least saved the tube. And Gareth is beside himself. He—I guess they said if he hadn't brought me in when he did it could've ended up a lot worse."

"I should've pushed you yesterday."

"It wouldn't have helped. I didn't want to lose another baby. And now..." July turned her head to the side and stared out the window.

"It's gonna be all right." The words left June's mouth before she could stop them. She didn't believe them—from July's flinch, she didn't either. Why did she bother with polite niceties with her sister? She shouldn't need them.

"How? How can it ever be all right now?" July pinned June with a fierce stare. "It's not like getting pregnant was easy and now it's going to be twice as hard. And Gareth's scared. He's not saying anything, but I can tell. He's going to say we need to stop. That a baby isn't worth the possibility of losing me. Maybe he's right."

June broke eye contact. She didn't have any answers. Didn't have any idea how to comfort her sister. How did you commiserate with someone who'd lost—twice now—the very thing she yearned for? At least July'd had the chance to experience a smidgen of that joy. June couldn't even say that. "I'm sorry."

July shrugged one shoulder.

They sat in silence for several minutes until a nurse knocked on the door and bustled in.

July flinched as the nurse adjusted her IV stand. "You should get home, June. Let Toby know I'm okay, please?"

"I thought..."

"Just go. Gareth will be back soon. Thanks for coming by."

June slid off the foot of her sister's bed, torn. Should she really leave? She didn't want July to be here alone...but if that's what she wanted...

"Okay. I'll come back tomorrow."

"Call first. I don't know how long they're going to keep me."

June trudged back to her car making a mental list of things to do that might help. She'd get in touch with Lydia and see if the class might arrange for some meals for when July got home. She should probably offer to house Mom and Dad if they wanted to come and be close. She'd clear that with Toby first though...maybe he'd save her and say no. She'd give Gareth a head's up as well. It'd be nice if she could convince Mom and Dad not to come, but that seemed...unlikely.

With the engine running, she grabbed her phone. She'd

text Lydia about the meals, then maybe this whole trip wouldn't seem like a waste. Flicking on her phone, she saw she'd gotten a text while she'd been visiting July. Why hadn't she heard the notification? She smiled when she saw it was from Lydia. The expression faded as she read.

I'm pregnant! Wanted u 2 know – will be u soon I know it!

"Great. Just great," June muttered and thumped her head against the steering wheel. Could this week get any worse? Where was God in all this? Probably too busy sending rain on the unjust to recognize that she could really use some help.

24

Gareth slipped his hand out of July's and shifted in the recliner. Was it even possible to be comfortable in the thing? July's deep breathing brought a smile to his face. At least she was resting. The nurses had been considerably less obtrusive than he'd expected. They came in and checked everything frequently, but they made little enough fuss that July went right back to sleep afterward. He wasn't quite so lucky.

When they'd arrived at the ER, he'd expected the usual hurry up and wait that you get with a trip to the emergency room. His heart still sped up when he recalled how they'd reacted when all the details had been given. Apparently you could get fast care when your emergency was life threatening. From admission to ultrasound to surgical prep had taken less than an hour.

He'd almost lost her.

The breath whooshed out of him. Chest tight, he stood and paced to the window, arms crossed over his chest as much for comfort as warmth. It simply couldn't happen again. Yes, he wanted children. Desperately. But not at the expense of July.

The whole point, really, was for them to be parents together. Without her...the point diminished considerably. And if the child was what took her from him, would he be able to forgive them? Or himself?

Why would God let this happen? There had to be some purpose behind it, didn't there? Was it simply to make it clear that they weren't supposed to have children? Or was there something else, something they were missing? And, at the end of the day, how could July not see that, at the very least, they needed to consider alternatives to starting a family?

Mouth set in a grim line, he settled back into the recliner and watched July's chest move up and down as she slept. He wasn't going to lose her. He couldn't.

"I'LL BE glad when we're home. Can't they speed this up at all?" July perched on the edge of the hospital bed, clutching her bag on her lap.

Gareth offered a weary smile. "The nurse said as soon as the doctor was free. I want to get you home, too. Four days in that recliner and I might need to seriously consider routine chiropractic care."

July frowned. "I told you you didn't have to stay."

"I know. But I couldn't leave you here alone." He hadn't meant to complain, but his back was aching. How long was this going to take? "Want me to go check?"

"No...you're right. They'll be here when they're here." July scooted back on the bed and set her bag aside. "Sit down."

"I'm good—just stretching."

The door swung open and the doctor strode in. "Hi, folks, sorry to keep you waiting." The doctor's gaze flicked down to July's bag and he chuckled. "I know you're anxious to go. Everything looks good, your incision is healing nicely, though I still wish we'd been able to do everything laparoscopically. You'll want to take it easy for another week – no heavy lifting, try not to do stairs more than twice a day, basic surgical recovery. They'll get you a sheet of instructions. And we'll call to schedule your next follow-up. Any questions?"

July glanced at Gareth.

He shook his head.

"I guess only one. When can we try again?"

Did she seriously ask that? She'd lost her mind. "Jules... don't you think..."

"No, no, it's a reasonable question." The doctor smiled. "I'm going to recommend you wait at least three, four months. There'll be a prescription for birth control with all your paperwork."

Gareth nodded. Good. That gave them some time to talk. Maybe he'd be able to get her to see reason.

～

"ARE you sure you're up to this?" Gareth settled next to July on the bed as she struggled to pull on khakis.

"I miss going to church. And I'm starting to feel trapped stuck at home. I know I'm not up to heading back to work yet, but I do think I can handle a morning out of the house. Especially since I'll be sitting the whole time."

"All right. If you're sure. But the minute you start to hurt or feel tired, let me know and we'll leave. Okay?"

"Okay."

Gareth watched her for a minute as she finished dressing. She looked like she was doing all right. "I'll go hop in the shower and get ready. You wait here and I'll help you downstairs."

He hurried through his shower, taking less time than usual. It'd be just like July to try and go downstairs on her own. She'd probably be fine, but he didn't want to risk it. Sure enough, when he went back into the bedroom, towel wrapped around his waist, she was gone. He huffed out a breath. He hurried to dress, running his fingers through his hair instead of the usual care he took to style it, and rushed downstairs.

July was sitting at the kitchen table sipping coffee. She was pale. He narrowed his eyes.

"Are you *sure* you're up to this? You already look worn out."

"I'm fine. Really." She took another sip from the mug and set it on the table. "Ready when you are."

Gareth pressed his lips together. He wanted to get out of the house too, but was this a smart idea? They'd only been home two days. He didn't want her to take longer to heal because they pushed it. And if he was honest, he wasn't ready to be in God's house. There were too many unanswered questions running through his mind, and praying hadn't helped answer any of them. What good would being at church do? If God had forgotten them, what was the point?

"Hey. You all right?"

He gave a start. "Yeah, fine. Lost in thought there for a minute. Let's go."

25

June let her eyes drift open. Toby had finally given up trying to wake her and gone downstairs. She'd tried to go back to sleep but failed. She should get up, go to church. She didn't want to. All those people with perfect lives. With everyone in the class expecting—everyone except her and July at least—it was an exercise in fortitude to get through the hour without saying something she couldn't take back. All they did was complain. So they were nauseous. So what? They had a baby growing in them, a little discomfort wasn't such a hard price to pay. June would give anything—anything at all—to trade places with them.

She suspected July'd be there today as well. June had gone to visit a few times while July was in the hospital, but it was hard. She'd had such terrible thoughts about July being pregnant and then, for this to happen...in many ways June felt responsible. If she hadn't had those thoughts, would this still have happened? Of course it would. It was ridiculous to think otherwise. And yet...why couldn't she have been happy for her sister? Then maybe she would've been welcome when it came time to try and offer comfort.

"Hey. You're awake." Toby came in holding a cookie sheet with a steaming mug and a plate balanced on it. "Thought maybe you could use a little breakfast."

June scooted to a sitting position, one corner of her mouth poking up. "That's sweet. Thanks. What've we got?"

Toby balanced the tray on her lap and sat. "Pancakes and coffee. Your favorite."

"Mmm. Thanks." June sliced a pancake into bites. "This is good."

He grinned and shifted, stretching his legs out in front of him and leaning against the headboard. "Wanna play hooky today? We could drive down to Williamsburg and walk around, enjoy the spring day, maybe have dinner at that tavern there on the main street before heading back?"

"Really?" Her heart leapt. Skipping church wasn't like him —could he possibly understand what she was going through?

"Really. You've had some hard knocks over the last couple weeks—more than that, if we're being honest. A day away from it all is never a bad thing. It clears the head. Maybe we can both get a little perspective."

She could use some perspective. Being angry with God made the ache in her heart hurt worse, but she couldn't stop. It was all so unfair. "Sounds perfect."

"Cool. Take your time eating. When you're ready, we'll go. But the name of the game is relaxed. So if we don't make it all the way down there because we find someplace we want to stop, then so be it."

June smiled and stabbed another bite of pancake. "That really is perfect. You're the best."

THE DAY WAS LOVELY. Even the two and a half hour drive on the interstate was pleasant. They didn't talk about anything in particular, carefully avoiding any mention of babies or June's job. They grabbed a quick lunch on their way to the Williamsburg Visitor Center, then spent the rest of the day following in the footsteps of the American Revolution. They finished the day with dinner at Chowning's Tavern before hopping back in the car for the trip home.

As the dashed white lines zipped along the side of the car, June looked over at Toby. "Thanks, hon. This was exactly what I needed."

He smiled and took one hand off the wheel, resting it on her leg. "I'm glad. I know you've been down lately. Between your job and the Clomid not working and July. But I also know we're going to get through this."

She frowned, turning to look out the passenger window. "How do you know? I want to believe that—I do—but I can't figure out how. Sure, Anthony's gone at work but there are already mutters in the hallway when I pass certain offices. He and his HR henchwoman did a lot of damage to my reputation that I don't know how to fix."

"I'm sure it'll blow over once the guy's been gone awhile. Just give it time."

June groaned. "Add to that...when we decided to try, I knew we were going to have no problem starting a family. Now? I don't even know if I can face trying to decide what to do next."

"What do you mean?"

"Where do I start?" She ran a hand through her hair. "We can try the Clomid again, but even Dr. Strong isn't overly optimistic about its chances based on the way the first round went. Which means we'll probably need to consider a reproductive endocrinologist. How do you even choose one? And once you do, how do you wade through all the options to figure out what you're willing to do?"

Toby shrugged. "Seems pretty straightforward, you do what the doctor thinks is going to be successful."

"I wish it was that simple. But I'm pretty sure I'm not okay with doing IVF. Do you believe, truly believe, life begins at conception?"

He gave a short nod.

"Me too. And the reading I've done...well you're making babies and then destroying some based on probabilities. I can't do that."

Toby was quiet for a long time. "I guess I hadn't thought about it that way."

She sighed. "Neither had I, until I started researching. Sometimes I wish I hadn't read as much as I did...but now, I can't see how I'd justify it. Or live with myself."

"Aren't there any options? A way to do it ethically?"

Were there? She hadn't read any—but she also hadn't kept researching once she realized how IVF really worked. "I'll have to look into that. If we get that far."

"What do you mean?"

"I guess I don't see the point. God made me this way. Why? I have no clue—there's another point I don't see, honestly. Why make someone broken like this and still give them the desire for children? It seems almost cruel. Taunting. Especially when the whole point of women being made the way they are is so that they can reproduce. So what purpose do I serve?"

"June." Reproach filled Toby's voice. "God has a purpose for all of us—we're made in His image."

"He made Adam and Eve in His image. Then the fall happened and now we're twisted by sin. So are we made in His image still? Or is the damage to some of our bodies a result of sin? Either way, it's pretty clear that at a minimum God allowed me to be made broken and useless. What possible purpose could He have for someone like that?"

Toby swallowed but said nothing. June watched as his hands tightened around the steering wheel. What was he thinking? She should have kept her mouth shut—no question

—but she had to talk to someone about it. July and Lydia were both out of the running. July had too much on her plate and Lydia...no one who was pregnant that easily could possibly understand. Lydia would probably at least try, but at the end of the day she'd be likely to spout the same nonsense Pastor Brown had. Have faith. How was she supposed to do that?

"Maybe we should go talk to the pastor."

"Why? He's just going to say that the rain falls on the just and the unjust or some other cliché designed to remind me that Christians aren't supposed to feel anything other than happy."

"He's not like that. You know he isn't. And...if you really believe what you just said, that God somehow made a mistake when He made you?" He looked over at her, concern evident on his face. "That's serious...and it worries me."

June blinked back tears and turned to stare out her window. Definitely should have kept her mouth shut. A tear slipped down her cheek. Why didn't anyone understand?

SHE COULDN'T DO THIS. June stared at the Pastor's house from inside her car. What was Toby thinking? He'd set up this appointment without even asking about her schedule. Not that she had anything else to do on a Monday night, but she'd rather be at home with her feet up. Or getting her teeth cleaned. Just because her life served no useful purpose didn't mean she was next in line for a suicide watch. It just meant... something. She had no idea what, but not that. The front door opened and Mary Brown waved at her. Dang it. Now she was stuck. She gave a half-hearted wave in response and grabbed her purse. Toby would pay for this somehow.

"So good to see you again, June." Mary wrapped June in a tight hug before pulling her inside.

June's smile was flat. "Thanks for squeezing me in. You didn't have to do that. Toby's overreacting."

"Nonsense. We didn't have anything else planned tonight and it's always lovely to have some time to chat with friends of Lydia's. Paul's in his study, do you mind if we join him in there?"

"Sure. Whatever." June followed Mary into a cozy room off the entry hall. It was exactly what a study should be—lots of books, a leather couch, a desk, and some arm chairs.

"Can I get you something to drink? Tea or coffee maybe? It's still getting a bit nippy at night." Mary hovered in the doorway.

"I'm fine." July sat on the couch and clutched the handles of her purse.

"Paul?"

"I've got water here. Give me one minute and I'll be ready." He looked back at his laptop and typed.

Mary settled next to June on the sofa with a gentle smile. "Ever since she ran into you at the mall, Lydia's been full of chatter about her new friend June. I'd hoped to have more time to get to know you at the women's brunch, but those things are always crazy. Sometimes wearing the pastor's wife hat means I don't get to enjoy things like I want."

"I was surprised how much Lydia and I had in common...it was nice to get to know her better." Not that they had anything in common anymore. But at least it'd been fun while it lasted.

"There." Paul snapped the lid of his laptop closed and moved from behind the desk to one of the chairs in front. "Sorry about that. I've found if I don't complete my thoughts when I have them, I end up losing them completely by the time I get back."

June chuckled. "I'm like that at work."

"So, what brings you here tonight?" Paul leaned back and propped an ankle on his knee.

"I figured Toby would've filled you in on that."

"He mentioned a few things, but I find it's always better to hear it directly." Paul folded his hands in his lap and gave her an expectant look.

This was ridiculous. She didn't need to be here. Nothing was going to help—it wasn't as if either of the Browns were going to be able to understand or offer anything other than platitudes. Gripping her purse, June stood. "This is a mistake. I'm sorry for wasting your time—Toby's just...over concerned."

"Oh please don't go." Mary patted the couch. "It's clear you're hurting about something. Why don't you at least let us try to help? If nothing else, we can pray with you before you go."

Like that was going to help. If God wasn't listening to her prayers, why would He listen to prayers about her? Still, Mary's earnest compassion had her sinking back down with a sigh.

"Toby and I have been trying to start a family. It's not going well...we're going to end up needing medical help, probably beyond what my regular doctor can do. Everyone else seems to have no trouble getting pregnant—it's what women are designed to do. But I'm broken. And several people have reminded me that God went out of His way to make me this way on purpose. I don't understand why. Why would He do that?"

Mary and Paul exchanged a look.

Paul cleared his throat. "I don't imagine I helped any with my comment in the hall of the hospital. I've been kicking myself ever since—but I didn't realize how much that must have hurt. First, let me apologize. I usually make it my policy not to comment on the deeper issues of faith in situations where there can't be extended discussion. I should have held to that."

June shrugged. "Maybe I shouldn't have asked then, either. I'm not sure what I expected you to say."

"The sovereignty of God is something I think everyone wrestles with. I still wrestle with it. We're created to want answers, to understand the whys of everything around us. But we're also told that God is working out His plan, a plan where only He has all the details. Throw in the seeming conflict between free will and God's omniscience and you have a puzzle that no one can fully unravel." Paul turned and grabbed the glass of water from behind him on the desk.

"So, essentially, you're saying accept that there's a reason and be done with it?"

"No, not at all." Mary shook her head. "I don't even think God asks us to sit back and be done with it. He wants us to struggle with it, to think about it, and, most of all, to *pray* about it. He reveals Himself to us when we ask."

"I *have* asked." A tear slipped down June's cheek. She scrubbed it away.

"Did you listen for His answer?" Mary leaned forward, her expression earnest.

June opened her mouth to say, "Yes, of course." And stopped. Had she listened? Did she ever listen? Or did she consider prayer a one-way street? She snapped her mouth shut.

Mary nodded. "I think we all fall into that habit. Throwing our prayers out there like drowning men screaming for help without ever looking around to see if He's thrown us a life preserver."

"Beyond that, we have to question our starting point. Do you believe that God is good?" Paul spun the now-empty glass in his hands and held June in his gaze.

Did she? A year ago, she would have quickly said she did. Now? "I don't know."

Paul pursed his lips. "That's the place to begin, then. You have to decide what you believe about the nature of God before you can decide how to proceed. If God is good, then He can—and will—use your brokenness, whatever form that takes because we're all broken in some way—for your good and His glory. It may not be the way you want or expect. You may not even think, at first, that it *is* for your good, but over time He'll reveal Himself if you let Him. If God isn't good, all bets are off and people suffer and are broken for no purpose beyond His cosmic entertainment."

June studied her toes.

He scooted forward in his chair so he could catch her gaze. "Ask yourself this: what purpose does Jesus serve if God is not good?"

26

"Do you believe God is good?" June blurted out the question as she and July rocked in the porch swing on the back deck of July's house.

July didn't hesitate. "Yes."

"Even after your miscarriage? And the ectopic? And how weird things have been with us lately?"

July nodded. "I can't say I love that any of those things have happened. But I believe there's a purpose behind them, because I believe that God delights in giving his children good things. The miscarriage, even the ectopic, brought Gareth and me closer together. They've brought me closer to God. Maybe I would've preferred to grow a different way, but if that's what it took to get me here..." She shrugged.

Could she say the same thing? June breathed in the spring air and let her gaze wander over the crocuses and daffodils that were beginning to spear through the mulch covering the garden.

July bumped June's shoulder with her own. "Why do you ask?"

Did she dare admit it out loud? If she was going to reclaim the relationship she and July had before their attempts at starting a family created a rift, she had to. She had to be willing to risk hurt again. Her sister was worth that, right? "I...It's something Pastor Brown asked me. I'm not sure how to answer it, frankly. I want to say yes. I want to believe that I believe God is good. But why would a good God make me this useless? My body is broken and its problems have driven a wedge between you and me...and if I'm honest, between me and Toby, too. Why would God do that to me?"

"Was it really God who did it?" July kicked the deck, making the swing rock a little harder.

June knit her brow. "Who else would've done it?"

"It's possible God made your body broken. That one I'll give you. Though I suspect it's more because we're no longer born in the perfect bodies God intended us to have—so I'd lay that firmly at the feet of original sin. Everything else though...that's all reaction to your circumstances. No one controls that but you."

June flinched as the words pierced her heart. July wasn't wrong...but why hadn't June realized it herself?

July rubbed June's leg. "Don't worry. You're not alone. I struggled with it in the hospital—but I had the benefit of extended hours with nothing to do. I kept my mind busy trying to process the fact that the large majority of my mental anguish was a result of how I chose to respond to the obstacles in my life. I'm choosing to believe that God's plan is going to be better than mine. Right now, I have to choose it several times a day."

June's mouth quirked up. "Is it getting any easier?"

"A little. This is helping." July let her head drop onto June's shoulder. "I've missed you."

"Me too."

∾

JUNE POKED her head into the office and smiled. Toby had his ear buds in and was muttering to himself as he pounded on the keyboard. What game was he playing? She crept into the room and snuck around behind him, getting momentarily dizzy as she watched him spin the vantage point of his character on the screen.

She leaned in and kissed his cheek. "I'm back."

Toby jolted and hit a key, bringing up the menu. He tugged out the ear buds with a chuckle. "Scared me. You have fun?"

"Yeah, it was nice." June swiveled his chair so she could settle in his lap. "I love you, you know that?"

He grinned, lowering his mouth to hers. "I heard something like that once. But it's always nice to hear again." He cocked his head to the side. "Good talk?"

She nodded. "I think we're back on level ground. Maybe not exactly where we were—but it's better, more purposeful. I'd always taken it for granted that we'd be friends because we were twins. Now I know we're friends because we want to be, not simply because we're sisters."

"That's fantastic."

June swallowed the lump forming in her throat. "I want to apologize for my poor coping skills the last several months. I'm gonna work on it...I can't promise miracles, but I'll try. I don't want to break what we have any more than I already have."

"We're not broken. Maybe there are a few new dings in the paint job, but underneath is solid as ever. We'll get through this."

She kissed his nose and slid off his lap. "I'll let you get back to the game—dinner in about an hour, 'k?"

"Got it."

June watched as he put the ear buds back in and hammered away at the keyboard. He was exhibit 'A' for ways God was good. She wasn't going to let herself lose sight of that again. Her faith had departed...but what was it the verse said? Joy comes in the morning. So until that new day dawned, and God brought back her faith, she would choose to believe that God was good. All the time.

WANT A FREE BOOK?

If you enjoyed Faith Departed and would like to read another book of mine, you can receive a free e-book simply by signing up for my newsletter here:
   http://bit.ly/2goAGvf

Keep reading for a sneak peek at book two in the Remnants series, Hope Deferred.

SNEAK PEEK OF HOPE DEFERRED, REMNANTS BOOK 2

Hope Deferred, Remnants Book 2
By Elizabeth Maddrey

"I've done all I can." Dr. Strong tented her fingers.

June swallowed the lump in her throat. It wasn't a surprise, not really. But the verdict still left her breathless. "So now what?"

"You'll want to find a reproductive endocrinologist. I'll make a copy of your file for you, hopefully that'll keep you from having to re-do three cycles of Clomid before moving on to something more likely to work."

June nodded. If only it was really that easy. She couldn't just go to an RE. Even with a referral from Dr. Strong, her insurance was going to fight it. And if they didn't pay...would Toby even consider it?

"Do you have someone you recommend?"

Dr. Strong shook her head. "Not really. It's not my specialty —and different insurance companies cover different medical groups. You tell me who your policy is most likely to work with and I'll write the referral to them."

"That's easy. No one." June huffed out a breath. "Sorry. I'll have to read through everything again, but I'm fairly sure they're not going to cover anything."

"Then I'd recommend choosing someone whose office is easy to get to first thing in the morning. You'll be making daily, or at least every other day, visits for ultrasounds during treatment." The doctor tapped a pen against her desk. "Tell you what, I'm going to fill out the form but leave the practice name blank. That way, once you decide where you're going, you can just fill it in. Saves you another office visit with me."

"Thanks." June watched as Dr. Strong scribbled on a pad of paper. How was she going to convince Toby?

June's head fell back against the top of her desk chair. Why couldn't insurance companies just write in plain English? Her pulse throbbed in her temples and words continued to swim in front of her eyes, despite the fact that she was no longer looking at her computer screen. Her eyelids drifted shut. At least...at least what? Her mind went blank. Surely there were blessings to count somewhere?

"There she is, my beautiful bride." Toby's lips brushed across her forehead.

"Hi, sweetie. How was your day?" June flicked her eyes to the computer screen—it had gone blank. Thank goodness for screen savers. The conversation about medical treatment to start a family could wait for a little while. At least until she got her thoughts together.

"Eh." He shrugged. "You know how it is. How was your day off?"

Or maybe it couldn't wait. "Fine...I had a consultation with Dr. Strong."

Toby ran a hand through his hair. "Oh?"

"Yeah. I should have mentioned it—meant to, in fact—I just never figured out how. Then I thought it'd just be easier to tell you once I knew what she had to say. I'm sorry."

He sank into his chair and leaned forward, elbows on his knees. "Okay. I guess. So what did she say?"

June sighed. It was better to rip the band-aid off, right? "She can't do anything else for us. It's time to see a specialist if we're going to keep trying."

Toby nodded but said nothing.

June watched him. What was he thinking? The wheels were spinning behind his eyes, but his expression stayed blank. "We don't have to talk about it now. Or even do anything about it right away."

"How are you doing?"

June drew her eyebrows together. He wasn't mad that she'd forgotten to mention the appointment? Or that they were going to have to pay for this out of pocket? "Um...okay, I guess. Disappointed. But I'm honestly starting to get used to that. This last year has left a layer of discouragement over most of my life that's thicker than the dust on the bookshelves."

The corner of Toby's mouth quirked up. "Is that a hint that I need to dust more?"

"You know what I mean."

"So, just disappointed?"

What was he getting at? "Not *just*, no. But I haven't sorted through everything yet—processed it, I guess. I...honestly, I was more worried that you were going to be angry."

He rolled his chair closer to hers and took her hand. "I'm sorry."

"There's nothing for you to be sorry about. As far as we know, all our problems are my fault. If anyone needs to be sorry, it's me. I know you didn't sign on for a broken wife."

He squeezed her hand. "That's not what I meant—and you're not broken. But we'll come back to that." He cleared his throat and waited until their eyes met. "I'm sorry that I've made you feel like you can't—or shouldn't—talk to me about this. I don't want you to only worry that I'm going to be angry when you're hurting."

"Oh." June offered a slight smile. "Thanks."

"I love you. Kids or no kids. When I asked you to marry me, I signed on to be your husband and spend the rest of my life with you. Anything else is gravy." He stood and kissed her forehead. "Why don't I see what I can scrounge for dinner? Then afterward, we can tackle the nightmare of the insurance website and see what we can figure out."

June's mouth dropped open as he left the room. He was taking this so well...had her impressions from the last four months been that far off? After their first failed cycle on Clomid in April, he'd been so insistent that they wait until June to try again. Then when that cycle failed, he'd pushed for another break before a third try. She'd assumed he was going to want an even longer break now that he was going to have to be more actively involved in the process. Maybe he didn't understand how much more he was going to have to do? Even if he didn't, she was going to savor having him back on her side for as long as it lasted.

THANK YOU!

I hope you enjoyed *"Faith Departed"*! I need to ask you a favor. Would you help others enjoy this book too?

Recommend it. Please help other readers find this book by recommending it to friends in person and on social media.

Review it. Reviews can be tough to come by these days. You, the reader, have the power to make or break a book. Loved it, hated it – I'd just enjoy your feedback. Please tell other readers what you thought about this book by reviewing it at one or more of your favorite retailers or social media sites.

My goal is to have 100 honest reviews. Will you help me reach that goal?

If you'd enjoy reading another book of mine, for free, I'd love for you to join my monthly newsletter mailing list. Sign up and get a book as my thank you. The form is located here http://bit.ly/2g0AGvf

And I'd love for you to connect with me on Facebook: http://www.facebook.com/ElizabethMaddrey

Thank you so much for reading *"Faith Departed"* and for spending time with me.

In gratitude,
Elizabeth Maddrey

AUTHOR'S NOTE

The years my husband and I spent struggling with infertility were some of my darkest days. I've never felt so alone, broken, useless, and abandoned. Since starting a family is supposed to not only be relatively straightforward but also somewhat personal and private, the isolation and inability to share with anyone still haunt me. This book has been percolating in my head for quite some time, but it's the hardest story I've ever tried to write. It's my dearest hope, if you are struggling with infertility (or have in the past), that this book has helped you remember that you're not alone. If infertility has not been a personal struggle, I hope June and July's story has given you a glimpse into the heartache that it brings.

No book comes to be without the help of many, many people. As ever, I'm grateful to Lynellen Perry at HopeSprings Books for her encouragement and editing. I'm also indebted to my critique partner Janice Elder, and my beta readers Wayne Greene and Rachel Fischer. My husband's support of my writing endeavors is a continual blessing—I couldn't produce anything intelligible without his riding herd on the boys and giving me a few hours of silence each week. Above all, I'm grateful to God for giving me words and stories to write. May these efforts be pleasing to Him and used for His glory.

RESOURCES

Whether you are just beginning to suspect something is amiss in your desire to start a family or you're well into infertility treatment, the book *Taking Charge of Your Fertility* by Toni Weschler is an incredible resource. This book gives a thorough explanation of how a woman's body works (or is supposed to work) and explains in detail how temperature monitoring can help you understand and identify any issues you might be having.

Resolve.org is the home of the National Infertility Association. Their website has a wealth of useful information.

Though not specifically infertility related, the best book I've ever read on the subject of the problem of evil is Randy Alcorn's *If God is Good*. If this is something you struggle with, it's a worthwhile investment of your time.

I was blessed to work with a wonderful group of women to produce an infertility devotional study titled *A Walk in the Valley: Christian encouragement for your journey through infertility*. It is our hope that the stories and thoughts therein are an encouragement and blessing to all who read them.

DISCUSSION QUESTIONS

1. June feels betrayed when July keeps a secret – is she justified, or is she overreacting?
2. People make comments and offer advice to June that ends up being hurtful. Will this influence you to think more carefully about how you deal with others in your life? Why or why not?
3. Has anyone ever made a comment to you when you were struggling that wounded you? What did you do about it?
4. If you've dealt with infertility, what was the hardest aspect for you? The easiest?
5. If you've dealt with infertility, were you open about it with everyone you met? Just your family? Another group? What influenced your decision to share or not?
6. Do you think the circumstances in the book were easier or harder for June and July because they are sisters?
7. Pastor Brown says before we can try to understand why God allows bad things to happen, we first have

to decide if we believe God is good. Do you agree? Disagree?

8. What do you tell people when they ask you why God allows evil to continue?

9. If you could say one thing to June or July, what would it be?

10. Do you believe men grieve infertility as deeply as women?

ABOUT THE AUTHOR

Elizabeth Maddrey is a semi-reformed computer geek and homeschooling mother of two who lives in the suburbs of Washington D.C. When she isn't writing, Elizabeth is a voracious consumer of books. She loves to write about Christians who struggle through their lives, dealing with sin and receiving God's grace on their way to their own romantic happily ever after.

Visit her website at www.ElizabethMaddrey.com